A SCIENCE FANTASIA

Three short science fiction novels

Francis A. Andrew

Order this book online at www.trafford.com/09-0399
or email orders@trafford.com

Most Trafford titles are also available at major online book retailers.

Note for Librarians: A cataloguing record for this book is available from Library
and Archives Canada at www.collectionscanada.ca/amicus/index-e.html

Printed in Victoria, BC, Canada.

ISBN: 978-1-4251-9181-8 (sc)

ISBN: 978-1-4269-0858-3 (e-book)

Library of Congress Control Number: 2009932571

*We at Trafford believe that it is the responsibility of us all, as both individuals
and corporations, to make choices that are environmentally and socially sound.
You, in turn, are supporting this responsible conduct each time you purchase a
Trafford book, or make use of our publishing services. To find out how you are
helping, please visit www.trafford.com/responsiblepublishing.html*

*Our mission is to efficiently provide the world's finest, most comprehensive
book publishing service, enabling every author to experience success.
To find out how to publish your book, your way, and have it available
worldwide, visit us online at www.trafford.com*

Trafford
PUBLISHING®   www.trafford.com

North America & international
toll-free: 1 888 232 4444 (USA & Canada)
phone: 250 383 6864 ♦ fax: 250 383 6804 ♦ email: info@trafford.com

The United Kingdom & Europe
phone: +44 (0)1865 487 395 ♦ local rate: 0845 230 9601
facsimile: +44 (0)1865 481 507 ♦ email: info.uk@trafford.com

10 9 8 7 6 5 4 3 2 1

—A Tale of Two Planets—

Introduction.

The following text which you are about to read was confided to me for safe-keeping by a NASA "deep-throat" with the strict instructions that it was not to be publicly disseminated until the year 2072 – thirty two years after the events to which it refers. By the time this information appears, I will long have been out of this world, and I do not mean as an astronaut! I am now 90 years old, and taking advantage of the new invention of Time Lapse Web Pages, or, Internet Hibernation, as some would call it, I do hereby post the full account of the strange happenings between 2030 and 2032, and so make them widely available by Internet WakeUp Alarm set for 2072.

Sir Reginald Wosley
(Astronomer Royal)
Cambridge: 2040.

Dear Sir Reginald,

There must be as many "explanations" for the bizarre events of the years 2030 to 2032 as there are people attempting to account for them. Before you delete this email as simply just another of these, may I point out to you that I worked as a senior scientist in radio space communications at NASA during the period in which these events occurred.

Attached to this email, you will find the micronodes which will provide you with the full text of the radio messages that originally came across as incomplete and garbled. If you analyse these nodes with Linguistic Analyser, you will find that they proceed in logical sequence from the same articulations as the "garbled messages". The Voice Analyser on your PC will indicate that they emanate from the same vocal chords as

3

those on the original "garbled messages". So this eliminates fraud by mimic and fraud by same voice synthesising.

I must now account for my being in possession of the complete texts of these radio messages. During the years 2025 to 2030, I headed the NASA team which developed the highly sensitive, highly technical, and, above all, highly secretive Photon Communicator Device (PCD) This device uses photons to carry radio waves across space and results in audio communication messages which are 100 times sharper than the conventional methods of communication. They eliminate the need for communication satellites and/or relay boosters on orbital craft. So we knew exactly who was communicating with whom even though those doing the communicating did not know each other!! The other feature of this device was its highly sensitive receiver which could pick up signals sent by conventional means. So we heard absolutely everything!

The most obvious question then to ask is why we told our astronaut that radio communications between him and NASA would fail. Why did we not use the PCD? The answer is clear and perfectly logical. If we had maintained full communication with our astronaut after the damage that had been caused to both the Mars Orbital Satellite and the Mother Ship, then the cat would have been out of the bag concerning PCD and thus would have rendered it prematurely widely available. Already in existence at the time was the method of sending secret radio signals to and from Earth, but these relied on satellites orbiting the Earth and satellites orbiting the Moon or Mars. The PCD did away with the need for these satellites by carrying the signals on light beams with direct pinpointing ability. By adjusting the resonance of both the sound and light waves, the signal becomes undetectable until it reaches the Resonance Adjuster at NASA.

4

Next we come to the issue of how an amateur radio hack managed to pick up signals which other more technically sophisticated radio dishes could not. In order to keep our Mars mission top secret, we had devised a means by which only NASA could receive any signals from Mars. This meant relaying the signals through a satellite in geostationary Earth orbit – the pre-PCD system. The catastrophe on Mars had affected the system maintaining geostationary orbit of the satellite as the Mars relay satellite and the Earth relay satellite maintained each other in their respective orbits around their respective planets. This was the essential means by which we ensured that the signals between Earth and Mars were picked up only by NASA. The failure of the Mars satellite knocked the Earth satellite out of its original geostationary orbit and caused it to take up another geostationary position. Although only an amateur radio enthusiast, our "radio hack" had managed to invent a kind of booster receiving device which enabled him to receive the Mars messages. Due to the method of "pinpoint signaling" which NASA had developed, the radio waves were not receivable over a wide area. We at NASA however, were able to hear the conversations as one of the applications of PCD is to eavesdrop on other people's communications while maintaining the secrecy of our own.

NASA Deepthroat 2040.

CHAPTER 1.

I Belong Tae Glasgow.

Brogieside East was one of the most run-down areas of Glasgow. Many sneeringly referred to it as "the new Gorbals". Indeed, it was as though a part of the Gorbals had escaped the demolition work of the bulldozers in the latter part of the 20th century and had magically uprooted itself and taken refuge in Brogieside East.

Oh how it lived up to its name as "the new Gorbals!" It boasted the highest murder rate in Scotland. Drink, drugs and poor nutrition ensured that average life expectancy was a mere 55 years – presuming of course that your throat was lucky enough not to come into contact with the jagged edges of a broken bottle long before you made it even that far.

Over the decades a panoply of politicians had made promise after promise to solve what eventually was termed "the Brogieside Question". Yet "the new Gorbals" remained unbowed. It was not that those who decided to take on "Brogie" had willfully reneged on their commitments; they had been well-meaning and well intentioned. They had not broken their promises, it was Old Brogie who had broken the politicians. Prime Ministers, MPs, city councilors, secretaries of state for Scotland, social workers, sociologists, clergy of all denominations, pop stars, sports personalities and a host of other celebrities had tried their hand at Old Brogie and only ended up having their hands tied – sometimes quite literally! As the locals would say – "Naebody braks the Brogie, it's thems that end up broken on the Brogie." So long before 2030, most politicians and social "experts" had, Pilate-like, washed their hands of Brogieside. The stalwarts who continued to take a stab at it were a brave, rare and near extinct breed.

At 45 years of age, Stephen Miller told his wife Flora, that he had about 10 years of life remaining, presuming of course that he was not "bottlethroated" for his weekly Giro cheque which he collected on his trip to the Department of Social Security. Since the radio factory in Brogieside had closed in 2025, Miller had been out of work. The Taiwanese, the Japs, the Koreans and the Thais could all make radios much cheaper than the British could. Stephen Miller was highly skilled in his job – but it was his only skill.

"You'll have to train for something else, Steve, you'll simply have to" Flora often told him.

"How many times have I told you, I'm too old to retrain?" I've been doing this since I was a loon of 14", retorted Stephen.

"And another thing, Steve", continued his wife, "you'll have to stop smoking pot, it really solves nothing, and you're only damaging your health".

"Och woman, awa an bile yer heid wid yi", yelled Stephen. "You're a fine yin to speak considering you're hardly ever awa frae the bottle." It was both Stephen's and Flora's habit to break into the broad Scots dialect when their tempers were aroused. What Stephen had just instructed his good wife to do was to "go away and boil your head, would you?!"

"Here's our Wullie having just completed the first year of

a six year stretch for selling cocaine", said Flora. "Now where does he get that habit from? And he's only 19".

"Aye, and here's our Jimmy just about to start a six year stretch for drunken assault with a broken bottle on old Councilor Mathews", replied Stephen. " To think that he was only 13 at the time of the offence. Now where does he get his taste for the hard stuff from?"

"Even though we're one of the more respectable families in Brogieside", said Flora, "I think it's a mercy they're both incarcerated in the Brogieside Borstal. At least there they'll have something of an education."

"Huh! Who has ever managed to educate anyone in Brogieside?" shrugged Stephen. "Anyway, I've had enough of your whining Flora, I'm going down to the shed for a bit of peace and quiet."

"Why do you waste time on that hack radio?" asked Flora. "You'll never make a living out of it".

"It's a hobby", replied Stephen. "Every man is entitled to a hobby", he continued. "It takes my mind off the awful realities of our … eh….. existence – heavens, I almost said 'life'".

Off went Stephen to his own little world in the wooden shed at the bottom of their patch of ground that one could possibly call a "garden". There he listened in to people's private mobile phone conversations, and to the radio communications between police cars - which, almost needless to say, were seldom idle in Brogieside. Stephen had learned a lot during his near 30 years at the radio factory. He hoped he could invent some sort of device and make his fortune. Since his redundancy he had been working on a kind of booster device which would enable him to snoop all the better on radio and cell 'phone communications.

CHAPTER 2.

MARS AIN'T THE KINDA PLACE TO RAISE YOUR KIDS.

Terence Brayson was never supposed to have been the first person to step on to the planet Mars. In fact, Cynthia Dobson was to have been the first woman to mark the Martian soil with a human footprint. Terry was indeed to have been the first man to set foot on the Red Planet though not the first person. As Cynthia's second in command, he was to have followed her down the steps of the lander. The eight other crew members were then to have trundled down the lander's steps and on to the dusty Martian Cerberus Plains which are around 7 degrees north of the Martian equator.

The robots which had been sent to the Cerberus Plains over the previous ten years had certainly done a magnificent job. They had built an entire complex consisting of a radio telescope, optical telescope, a science laboratory and living quarters for the ten man crew who were to spend around two years exploring parts of the equatorial region of the planet.

Terry made his way to the living quarters and after filling it up with oxygen, he took off his pressure suit and went over to a dining table. He had derived no thrill from being the first human on Mars. In fact, all the excitement which he had nurtured over the past five years of intensive training,

training just for this very moment, had dissipated into the thin Martian atmosphere. Terry sat down at the table and at long last released his pent up emotions which he had been holding back for the past two hours. He fell into a fit of uncontrollable sobbing. He remained in this condition for at least fifteen minutes.

The astronaut had every reason for this extreme outburst. Something had gone badly wrong just prior to the lander separating from the mother ship. Terry had been the first to enter the lander craft. It was his job to bring it safely on to the planet's surface. The standard operating procedure had been for him to check that all systems were go just before the rest of the crew entered. While he had been engaged in these tasks, a most strange thing happened. There was an almighty explosion in the mother craft. Through the porthole, he saw that the oxygen supply had been damaged by the mysterious explosion and the crew members lay dead. To his absolute horror, he realised that he would have to land alone. Re-entry to the mother ship was out of the question – and in any case, all his friends had been killed by a combination of the explosion, the failure of the oxygen supplies and the toxic gasses which now filled the ship.

Just after landing on the Cerberus Plains of Mars, Terrence Brayson looked up into the red and blue Martian sky and witnessed a huge explosion – the mother ship was now no more. He had made his way to the radio dish and once inside, told NASA the appalling news. NASA assured him that within 18 months to two years, either he or his body would be taken back to Earth. A rescue mission would be dispatched within a week. Meanwhile, he had sufficient oxygen, food and water to sustain him for those two years. He also had suicide pills! Even if he survived the two years on this cold, dead planet, what was life anywhere in the

Universe without Cynthia? He and Cynthia were to have been wed on their return to Earth.

"What am I supposed to do here all alone on this God-forsaken hell-hole of a planet?", he asked himself. Communication between himself and NASA would not now be possible as the relay system and booster had been located aboard the ill-fated mother ship and, a few hours after the mother ship had blown up, the communication satellite strayed from its original geostationary orbit which had been directly over the Cerberus Plains and took up a new position nearer to the Martian north polar cap. He thought again of his dead companions and started sobbing once more. He thought of Cynthia and fell on the floor and banged his fists crying out "my God, my God, why hast thou forsaken me?" His faith wavered as he pondered as to why fate should have dealt him and Cynthia such a cruel and merciless blow. Their lives had been one of innocence and purity. Against the modern trends, they had promised not to "know" each other in the biblical sense until they were married. He thought on the scripture texts "my ways are not your ways" and "God works in mysterious ways". All he could do was to say "yeah, yeah, yeah".

In the dining area, he cooked himself a meal of bacon, eggs and mushrooms. He didn't really have much of an appetite, but he knew that he had to eat to keep his strength up. The sun was now setting and he decided that in the morning he would start exploring his surroundings. But first, he needed a good night's sleep. Like the Earth, Mars rotates each twenty four hours, so sunrise and sunset would be similar to what they were on Earth. That, however, would be about all Mars could offer Terry as a "home from home".

When Terry stepped out of the living quarters and on to the Martian surface, he was on time to see the beautiful

Martian sunrise. The sun shone dimmer and colder here than it did on Earth. As a boy, Terry had been fascinated by the stories he had read about Mars. Was there any form of life on the red planet? Had there once been a thriving civilization on Mars? Various spacecraft which had been sent over the past seventy years to investigate this planet had beamed back to NASA pictures which seemed to show "anomalies" on the planet's surface: faces, buildings, pyramids, sphinxes and a host of monuments. Many sensationalist books had been written on the "artificial structures" and "artifacts" on Mars. Terry had devoured these books and believed (or perhaps had wanted to believe) that Mars was as much an archeologist's, historian's and biologist's paradise as it was a geologist's.

As Terry surveyed his surroundings, he saw no pyramids, no buildings apart from the ones the robots had constructed, no monuments, no artifacts, and certainly no little green men. What lay before him in all directions was a bleak, cold, lifeless, rock-strewn landscape. He went over to the radio dish and entered its operating section. He thought he would try and make some sort of contact with NASA however feeble the signal might be.

"It must be possible to send and receive signals from NASA on this thing even without a relay booster", thought Terry. "I'll give it a whirl".

Chapter 3.

Operator, hello, hello.

Terry sent the following message: "The robots have done a good job. Everything here is functional. Suicide is not an option and I'm going to make the best of things here until I am rescued. I'm going to start the biology experiments and see if things will grow on the Martian soil".

Terry realised that he would have to be positive. There was no use crying over spilled milk. No amount of moping would bring Cynthia back to life. And had not Cynthia told him that if anything were to happen to her, he would have to assume full command? Now he would respect both Cynthia's instructions and her memory. Terry set himself to work.

In his rickety wooden shed in Brogieside, Stephen Miller picked up a somewhat garbled signal on his radio: "Robots.... job. Suicide is not an option....make best .....experiment.... things....grow on....soil."

"My God"! exclaimed Miller. "Who is reading my thoughts?" Miller, after surveying the bleak prospects for his miserable life, had contemplated a drug overdose as a way of getting it all over and done with.

The recording equipment that Miller had attached to his dish was on. He played back the strange message many times wondering what it all meant. He stopped himself from emptying the contents of a needle into his arm and decided to radio back.

"Who are you? Where are you? Please give more details".

On the Cerberus Plains of Mars, Terry Brayson picked up the following signal: "Who...you? Where...? Please.... more details". Losing even more interest in his suicide pills, Brayson signaled back: "NASA. Have you the brains of a worm.? Have you been living down some hole? You know perfectly well who I am?"

Stephen Miller picked up the signal: "Ass....worm.... down a hole. You know who I am?" Miller signaled back: "Sorry I don't know you. Please clarify. I have no proof but may I just have you know that my name is Stephen Miller and I need psychiatric help desperately"

The signal that Brayson picked up a few minutes later came over like this: "....don't know you. I...... Harvard..... Professor Sean Miles...Psychiatry Department...help."

"Good Heavens!" thought Brayson. "Is this a chance signal or have they assigned me a psychiatric counselor?"

Brayson signaled back: "Sorry about the remark about worms and holes. That reminds me though, I must now begin the biology experiments and see if gardens grow on Mars!"

Miller received the message: "Sorry..... worm holes.... gardens grow".

Miller radioed back: " I'll get some seed and will start planting and hope they will be saved from being eaten by worms. I'll try and make my garden grow".

Brayson received a message which he interpreted as: "....start planting......saved by wormholes......".

Miller to Mars: "Who are you?"

Brayson to Earth: "I am Terrence Brayson. I am an astronaut stranded on Mars. I feel like the loneliest man in the Universe. All the crew including my fiancé have been killed. Oh how I need your psychiatric help. A professor of psychiatry is just what I need".

And Miller heard the following: "I am Ernest Gray...... Stanford University....professor of Psychiatry.....".

On leaving the radio observatory complex, Terry looked up at the pale Martian sky and wondered about wormholes. Astrophysicists were not sure if they existed. Theoretically, they were supposed to bend time and space and so enable anyone entering one to travel anywhere in the Universe in literally no time at all. He wished he could will one into existence and travel back to Earth. It was though, wishful thinking, and he soon came back down to Mars with a thump by realising that he would never come down to Earth with a thump! "How I wish I could swap places with 'Sean Miles'" mused Terry. And Stephen mused about how wonderful life would be if he could swap places with "Ernest Gray". Terrence Brayson looked up at the Martian sky and fantasised about wormholes. Stephen Miller looked down at his litter-strewn garden and worried about worms making holes in any seed potatoes he might plant there.

Chapter 4.

Brogieside and Cerberus Market Gardeners Ltd.

"What are you doing Steve?!" cried Flora as she saw the patch of scrubland they called a garden being cleared of its empty beer bottles. Miller explained all about the garbled radio conversations he had been having with his Stanford professor of psychiatry.

"Are you sure it's not the pot that's speaking to you?" she enquired. "Next thing is", she continued, "it'll be little green men from Mars".

"I'm no imaginin' anythin'", protested Stephen., and he played back the recordings of the conversations to her.

"I think your professor is telling you that gardening is psychologically therapeutic", she conjectured.

"That's why I'm having a stab at this piece of barren desert", replied her husband. "It's noo late April and just the right time to be planting the seed tatties".

Under the artificial heating and lighting in the greenhouses built by the robots on Cerberus, Terry Brayson was busy planting an assortment of fruits and vegetables on the Martian soil. "Professor Miles is right – gardening is good for the soul."

Stephen Miller was becoming something of a celebrity in Brogieside. His "garden experiment" had caught on. First people turned over their back yards and "greens" into gardens. Those who were not fortunate enough to have a bit of ground did what they could with box sills. The old "plots" were got back into production and even the earth in tracts of wasteland were starting to become fertile as people took the law into their own hands and staked their claim by fencing them off.

"Weel Stevie, they are designated 'public lands'. Now aren't we members of the public?"

"Aye Tammy. Naebody need worry aboot it. If the politicians dina care aboot us ordinary folks, we'll just hae tae start caring for oorsels", replied Miller in the Scots tongue.

It was not long before fairs and markets were appearing all over Brogieside. Sometimes the produce was paid for in cash, sometimes barter was the means of exchange. Stephen Miller had never planned or even dreamed that his little experiment would have had such far reaching consequences. Not only that, but his agricultural knowledge was soon recognised and his advise was asked for. In disputes over prices and exchange, it was his arbitration which was sought.

When little green things started to peep through the Martian soil, Terry Brayson excitedly claimed – "things do actually grow in the Martian soil." By September, he had excellent crops of potatoes, tomatoes, cucumbers, radishes, apples, oranges and grapefruit.

He radioed a message to Earth: "The soil is productive. I'm now thinking of livestock". However, he felt a pang of sadness sweep over him as he thought about how Cynthia would have been so thrilled with these experiments. Oh how he wished he could share his glee with her. She had always been convinced that Mars could be changed from the red planet to the green planet. Her great ambition had been to initiate the Genesis Experiment on Mars. She had envisioned giant orbital mirrors being used to reflect sunlight on to the polar caps and so melt their frozen waters. A wetter Mars, she concluded, would be a greener Mars. She was convinced of the viability of the terra-forming of the Red Planet. She had so much wanted to make Mars just like the Earth. It was a generally held belief among the astronomical community that Mars had indeed been like the Earth for a period of its ancient history – but something had gone badly wrong. Many theories abounded as to just what exactly had gone wrong. One theory held that a massive meteorite had struck the planet thus depriving it of its once thicker and more varied atmosphere. Another contended that Mars had once been a moon of a planet; this planet exploded and its debris formed the asteroid belt. Mars then became a planet in its own right and assumed its own orbit around the sun. Terry came to share Cynthia's dream of terra-forming Mars; together, as husband and wife they would share the task of bringing their dreams to reality and bring back to Mars its former Earth-like glory. It broke his heart that his tentative small scale efforts at terra-forming were being accomplished without Cynthia, but the memory of Cynthia and the strong conviction which he held that she would have wanted him to do what he was now engaged in doing served to perk him up and spur him on. "If I gave up out of grief", he thought, "Cynthia would be the first to give me a hard kick up the backside!"

As Terry stepped out of the greenhouse where his plants

were growing, his eyes strayed over to the horizon. He stopped in his tracks. "Did I see something move just now – or is my imagination playing tricks on my eyes?" He looked again but saw nothing. He concluded that it was all just a bit of wishful thinking.

"Professor Gray is now recommending livestock", Stephen told his wife.

"Sounds fine", replied Flora, "but we need grazing land".

"Tammy Crawford told me today that there were plenty of open spaces that could be cleared for sheep and cattle", said Stephen.

Many of the Brogieside residents got together, pooled their resources, bought some good top-soil and started to grow grass on various council sequestered allotments. Hardy breeds of sheep, goats and cows were soon grazing on them. Pigs and poultry were being bred in back yards and the local ad hoc fairs were thriving like never before.

Grass grew well under the huge glass domes which enclosed grazing fields for cows and sheep. These animals had been taken to Mars two years previously by unmanned spacecraft. They were maintained in a state of Deep Freeze Hibernation (DFH). Brayson wondered if they could really still be alive. He took them out of their cubicles and injected them with the wake up drugs. He was pleasantly astonished to see them slowly but surely struggle to their feet and to start munching on the grass. Five acres of pasture were enclosed in glass domes. The special type of glass developed by NASA ensured that the dangerous cosmic rays which easily penetrated the thin Martian atmosphere did not enter the "pasture lands". Like the other buildings in the area, the pasture lands were supplied with oxygen from massive containers placed nearby.

When Terry stepped out of the "pasture dome", his eyes

caught sight of an object moving on the horizon. This time he was not so convinced that his mind was playing tricks on him. "I'm sure that was a vehicle of some description". This time he was going to investigate. He set up a small digital telescope and embarked upon a survey of the entire horizon. He programmed the instrument to photograph the entire horizon as far as the telescope's range would permit.

When the photographs were analysed the following day, no anomalies were present in them – nothing but more of the same, the same bleak and barren landscape that surrounded the base. However, one photograph did make Terry pause for a moment. He looked more carefully at it. "This looks like a building of some description". He plotted its distance, got into the Marsmobile and decided to investigate. As he approached the object, his hopes were dashed – it was just a clump of rocks! Terry rebuked himself for not having realised that that was the interpretation he should have given it. "If there is such a thing as 'Martians'", mused Terry, "they will surely have made themselves known to me long before now". With that thought, he ended his day's work and went to the living quarters to relax. He watched *The Sound of Music* on the DVD player. The beautiful green Austrian fields depicted in this old classic helped take his mind away from the awful realities of Mars.

CHAPTER 5.

VARIETY IS THE SPICE OF LIFE.

Terry Brayson radioed this message back to Earth: "Hello Professor Miles. The flora and fauna are doing well here on Mars. I think it is now time to embark upon other scientific experiments. I'm going to start collecting and analysing rock samples. We need to obtain more information on the geological composition of the planet".

Back on Earth, Stephen Miller picked up the following distorted signal on his radio: "...flora ....doing well....analyse rock samples....need geological composition".

"How does this guy know my wife's name?" wondered Stephen. Anyway, I'm fascinated to find out what all this geology and rock samples is about.

"You've done a good job with the eh 'agriculture' of Brogieside, Steve" said Flora. "Don't push things too far", she warned him. "Be content with the way things have developed".

"Well, everything isn't money, you know. We need to consider the culture and education of the youth of Brogieside", replied her husband.

Flora laughed. "Oh sure, I can just see the Brogieside bottle - throaters deep in discussion over the subtle differences between one Brogieside rock and another!"

"We have to at least give this a try", retorted her husband.

"Now look", he continued, "I've given up the dope but I've still to see you get fully weaned off the bottle. If you gave up your drinking, I'm sure you'd adopt a more positive attitude to life".

Dr. Walter MacPherson, the President of the Geological Society of Glasgow looked hard and curious at his unexpected visitor. "We'd be quite happy to co-operate with your ..em... education committee, Mr. Miller as our Society has never made any kind of geological survey of the Brogieside. However, I'm sure you'll appreciate my concerns about venturing into that neck of the woods. It's not exactly too safe".

Stephen Miller then told his academic host about the great changes which had taken place in Brogieside and all of it having been accomplished on the initiative of its residents. He assured MacPherson that he and his survey team would have the protection of the "Brogieside Polis" ('polis' being the Glaswegian slang for 'police') a sort of private police force which had evolved to do the job that the official police were incapable of doing – protecting law abiding citizens.

Only one tentative field trip to Brogieside had been planned. The "Brogieside Polis" however had done such an excellent job in protecting the members of the geological expedition that a second one was planned. When the Brogieside youth actually took a keen interest in the work of the geological team members and even started analysing the rocks themselves and co-operating with the geologists by handing them rock samples, putting them into categories and cleaning them of their native Brogieside muck, field expeditions by the Geological Society of Glasgow became a regular sight in Brogieside.

When many of the Brogieside youth actually took more of an interest in the composition of rocks than in their use as projectiles to be aimed at peoples' heads, monthly lectures on geology were held in the new community centre in Brogieside.

"The results of our geological survey, Mr. Miller, show a high uranium content for the rocks in and around Brogieside", said Walter MacPherson during a visit to the Miller home.

"Could this be significant in any way?" asked Miller.

"Oh yes of course" replied MacPherson. "With hydrocarbons nearing depletion levels, the whole world must redouble its efforts in the way of nuclear power generation. And you've got the necessary raw material right under your very feet."

"So what exactly are you proposing, Dr. MacPherson", asked Miller.

"Tell me", said MacPherson, "are your electricity and fuel bills high?"

"You can bet they are", replied Flora.

"Then if all your fuel and energy needs were to be generated by a local nuclear power plant, your bills would be reduced to at least a quarter of what they currently are", said Macpherson.

"What about the radiation hazards from a nuclear power plant?" Stephen asked Professor Brian McKinley the head of the Department of Physics at Glasgow University. MacPherson had referred Stephen Miller to McKinley to discuss the matter further.

"Well now, Brogieside has been, let us say, 'radioactive' for millions of years", McKinley explained. "A nuclear power plant is going to add next to nothing".

McKinley then went on to debunk the scaremongering of the anti-nuclear lobby and informed his guest that of all the various sources of radioactivity, both natural and man-made, nuclear power stations gave off by far the least radioactivity.

"Furthermore", went on McKinley, "we in the Department of Physics at Glasgow University, are developing small scale nuclear powered generating stations. These essentially have two advantages; first of all they can be used for relatively small scale power generation such as would be required for factories and neighbourhoods – such as your own Brogieside. Secondly, their burn-up rate is so highly efficient that most of the Uranium 238 in common rocks can be changed to Uranium 235. So smaller amounts of rocks are required and the waste is almost negligible".

"I think you would like to build one in Brogieside", Miller guessed.

"Yes", answered McKinley, "at least on a temporary and experimental basis".

Terrence Brayson had accumulated a massive collection of Martian rocks. He radioed back to Earth: " Analyses of rock samples in the area around the base indicate a high uranium content. Uranium baring rocks are everywhere so there should be no problem building nuclear power generators to meet the energy requirements of future Martian colonies."

In his little wooden shack, Stephen Miller heard the following defective message come through: ".......uranium baring rocks...everywhere......no problem....nuclear power generators....meet energy requirements of future......".

"Even Professor Gray advises nuclear power", said Stephen to his wife.

"But he's a professor of psychiatry at Stanford University in the USA", objected his wife. "How would he be qualified to speak on nuclear energy?"

"He's an intelligent guy I'm sure", replied Stephen. "He must speak to his pals in the science faculty I would guess".

A few days later Brayson sent out another signal to his "psychiatric counselor" "Sean Miles": "As the Martian gravity is only half that of the Earth's, muscle mass tends to deteriorate. I shall now embark upon some physiological experiments in the sports complex and monitor the changes in fat to muscle ratio".

This is what Stephen Miller thought he heard: ".....muscle mass...deteriorates.....sports....changes.....fat to muscle...."

It was not long before Miller had persuaded some football stars from Celtic and Rangers to coach some of the Brogieside kids in "fetba". Within a short space of time, Brogieside Amateur Football Team were winning most of their matches against other Glasgow amateur teams. A sports club was built and professionals in basketball, volleyball, the martial arts and a whole array of sports now saw Brogieside as a means of gaining greater publicity for themselves. The relationship however was symbiotic; the Brogieside youth displayed their athletic prowess in any sporting endeavour they undertook and walked away with armfuls of cups, medals and trophies.

Brayson sent out another radio signal: "I will now start regular astronomical observations. The thin Martian atmosphere provides excellent viewing conditions. The telescope appears to be in good working order".

This is what Miller picked up: "....start regular astronomical observations....telescope ....order".

"What"! shrieked Flora. "He wants you to order a telescope?!"

"I don't see anything wrong with an astronomical society", Miller said.

A few months later, a dome type structure housed Brogieside Astronomical Society's 20 inch reflecting telescope.

Miller radioed to his mysterious friend: "We have now

got a 20 inch telescope in place. We do our viewing when the night sky is clear".

Here is what was picked up by Brayson: "....get a 20 inch telescope in your place....is that clear?"

"Oh my God" exclaimed Brayson. "Miles may be a good psychiatrist but he obviously knows nothing about astronomy. I'm using a 120 inch reflector here, for Heaven's sake".

Brayson radioed this message back: "Aquarius is prominent now. Try to photograph it".

Miller heard: "Aquarium....now. Photography...."

And so it came to pass that fish farming and photographic clubs sprung up all over Brogieside.

Brayson radioed his friend: "Will now point the radio telescope dish skywards and see what it produces.

Miller heard this garbled message: "....radio...dish.... products".

Brogieside radios were relatively crude devices, but they were affordable and they played the latest pop music!

Miller to Brayson: "Great pop music on the radios"

Brayson heard this: "....pop music grates on me".

Brayson to Miller: "Then try classical. Classical on Cerberus Plains is quite romantic".

And to Millers ears it sounded like: "....classical plainly cuts down on crime".

This was the toughest nut of all to crack – trying to get the Brogieside boys (and girls for that matter) to listen to Beethoven, Brahms and Mozart. But when some of the few enthusiasts that there actually were started playing recorded classical music rather than pop and rock in bus and railway stations and even in public toilets, the crime rate diminished yet further and a few classical music societies sprang up.

The botched and bungled messages between Earth and

Mars continued, and as they did, so did Brogieside improve in leaps and bounds. Here are a few more examples:

Brayson to Miller: "Sometimes I feel that these experiments are just bally hoo. Yet with a concerted effort I think Mars could become habitable. I don't want to paint too bleak a picture as I'm sure that if Mars could be warmed up, people could swim in artificial lakes and do all sorts of water sports. And it's cold enough for skiing all year round. The library in the communal area is fine but it could do with some more reading material – either conventional books or electronic ones. Giovanni Shiaperelli, the 19th century Italian astronomer, thought he saw canals on Mars. I see none – anyway that was his story. Was there ever intelligent life on Mars? But then, has there ever been intelligent life on Earth? Did any life at all ever exist on Mars? So far I see no sign of it. That of course does not mean it isn't there. Archeologists and paleontologists may yet find employment on the red planet. And then of course we'll have space tourists coming to Mars"

Soon, ballet schools, concerts, art schools, swimming baths, skiing resorts and libraries were flourishing in Brogieside. A historical society was set up to research the history of Brogieside. The rough locals of Brogieside co-operated with the academics of the history department of Glasgow University in uncovering Brogieside's interesting past. And what a wealth of information there was! No-one had ever dreamed that such a poor neighbourhood would have played host to such rich bygone years. Those assigned the task of digging canals to transport people and goods to and from Brogieside were told to look out for archeological artifacts and inform the newly formed Brogieside Archeological Society about them. Bones and fossils were to be carefully removed and sent for analyses to the Brogieside Paleontology Society. Space was soon found for tourist information centres and many of the Brogieside residents spruced up their homes to receive Bed & Breakfast guests who came to see for themselves what ordinary people in an ordinary neighbourhood could do if they really took their coats off to the job and rolled their sleeves up.

CHAPTER 6.

ALIEN VISITORS.

Terry Brayson often used one of the "Marsmobiles" for exploration of his surroundings and to extend his geological surveys. A drive of about twenty miles took him to within view of the huge Mon Olympus, the largest volcano in the solar system. It is 72 miles wide and its peak reaches a staggering 12 miles in height. Unfortunately the fuel and oxygen supplies of the Marsmobiles were insufficient for this range of extra vehicular activity, so Terry contented himself with viewing this massive geological feature from a distance. Terry was master of all he surveyed. Once again Terry thought he saw a vehicle moving in the distance. He also thought he saw a forest and buildings in the very far distance. This time he ignored all that and would not even bother to investigate. "I'm not going to be a slave to my imagination and let it send me on another wild goose chase again. I'll go on no more fools' errands." As he returned from his excursion and approached the precincts of the base, he stopped the vehicle and stepped out on to the Martian surface. The base was lit up with atomic power. Its light, its plants, its grazing animals stood in absolute and utter contrast to the rest of the cold, bleak and desolate Martian landscape. The robots had built the base, but one man had brought it to life.

For nearly two years, one man had sustained the living be-ings on it. One man had done the work of ten. He felt he had the right to be proud; he felt he deserved to pat himself on the back; he felt he had the right to high honours back on Earth and nothing less than a hero's welcome home.

One thing that Terry had failed to do was to render the robots functional. Try as he might they remained dead and motionless. He had tried all sorts of programming, but it was all in vain. "Perhaps they can only be controlled from Earth", he thought. Terry had devised computer programmes which would have got these steel monsters digging, mining, factory building and smelting the metallic ore in the Martian rocks. Why should he, a diminutive human being be performing back-breaking work while these hunks of metallic chunks remained idle. He wanted to put them to work and to work hard! They remained erect yet lifeless, like the stone statues of Easter Island, starring out into the vast dried up oceans of Mars. Their posture was as if they were at the ready to instantly obey without question any command given to them, but it was certainly not to be Terry's commands. Though they seemed to be expecting a command at any moment, the order never came, and eventually Terry gave up on them as a hi tech mausoleum. In his less kinder moments he would yell at them "you're a pile of worthless junk, a useless load of scrap metal."

As the rescue spaceship approached Mars, Terry managed to make contact. His mood began to change and he saw Mars in a completely different light. The sun seemed to shine brighter, the plants looked greener and the lambs frisked more merrily in their massive glass-covered fields. How he now felt about Mars was how he imagined he would have felt about it almost two years previously had the mission not aborted.

Improved communications now meant that Terry could keep in regular contact with the rescue ship. He gave detailed accounts of his two year stint on Mars, and these were relayed back to NASA. He also related to NASA via the ship's communication systems his mysterious conversations with "Prof. Sean Miles".

Oh the joy, oh the wonder, oh the sheer delight of seeing other human beings again! As Terry watched the hatch of the lander craft open and three astronauts emerge, he wondered if this was just another of those many dreams of rescue missions his sub-conscious mind subjected him to in his sleeping hours. As the four of them approached the base's living quarters, Terry still remained unsure as to whether he was awake or asleep. When they divested themselves of their pressure suits, two men and a woman were revealed to Terry.

"Hi, I'm Sheila Mitchell". "I'm Alexander Johnstone". "And I'm David Henderson".

"As we said during our radio communications, we'd like to spend a couple of days here", said Mitchell.

"I know you must want to get off this planet asap", added Henderson, "but we would really like to see with our own eyes, the wonderful work you've done here".

"NASA wants us to make a full report of our findings", said Johnstone.

"In fact, I would consider it an insult if you did not at least take some interest in my accomplishments here", said Terry rather haughtily.

For two days, Brayson, Mitchell, Johnstone and Henderson made a tour of the base facilities and went for excursions in the Marsmobile.

"You know Terry", said Johnstone, "we didn't expect to find you alive".

"If I may be blunt", said Mitchell, "I really thought we were coming just to pick up your dead body".

"Well, it hasn't been easy", Brayson explained to his three companions. "It has taken every ounce of my spiritual, mental and physical energy to do all this".

"You can feel justly proud", Henderson told him.

"You're a real cosmic Robinson Crusoe" said Mitchell.

Human nature is very strange. Though Terry had longed to get off of Mars, though he pined for Earth, though he was almost willing the rescue craft to increase its speed, he felt great sadness at having to leave all this, his creation, behind. He had ensured that there would be enough fodder and oxygen for the animals to survive until either the next manned or robotic mission came to the red planet to continue his work. He gazed upon his work and comforted himself by imagining this relatively small base expanding into cities and fields in the next ten to fifteen years. This, he conjectured, would be the first step in the complete transformation of Mars.

Once inside the rescue lander craft, Terry looked out over the Cerberus panorama for the last time. He took one last loving gaze at his model base. "Yes", he thought, "it is indeed the model for any grand project to make Mars a habitable world." Then all of a sudden, Terry saw something which caused him to freeze in horror. He really thought he was dreaming this time. "Surely my eyes are playing tricks", he told his three companions.

"I want you to watch this spectacle Terry", said Henderson.

Brayson watched in stunned shock and horror. "No! No! No! he yelled. Why! Why! Why! in God's name - Why!?" he screamed. "Can't you stop this? Have you no control? Cease this utter madness this instant!" But in spite all of Terry's pleading and imploring, the nightmare continued. Terry watched the ghastly spectacle for half and hour It was truly his very own dark night of the soul. The shock and horror had now given way to tears of grief. Brayson collapsed on the floor of the craft after Johnstone administered a sedative.

When Terrence Brayson woke up, he was aboard the mother ship which had now left Mars orbit and was speeding back to Earth.

"Don't ask any questions", warned Sheila Mitchell.

Commander Raymond Taylor told Brayson that under the 2012 National Security Act, he must neither ask questions about what he had seen nor relate it to anyone. "All will be explained in due course, once we are back on Earth", said the commander. "Regarding what you witnessed, keep your mouth shut now and for always", he continued in threatening tones.

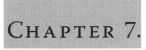

Chapter 7.

Those damned politicians.

Stephen Miller received yet another visiting delegation – but this time it was of a different kind. It was not composed of the usual scientists, philanthropists, technocrats, sports personalities, historians, archeologists and various other academics. Outside Miller's door stood the stern-faced Chief Constable of Glasgow, the Lord Provost of Glasgow, the MP for Brogieside, the MEP for South West Scotland and most of Glasgow City Council.

"Are you Lord Stephen Miller, Earl of Brogieside?" asked the Chief Constable.

"I am", was Miller's short reply. The Brogieside Historical Association in co-operation with the Department of History at Glasgow University and the office of Lord Lyon King of Arms, had discovered and resurrected an ancient earldom to which Miller was the closest in blood line. Miller had been left wing and republican all his life. When he accepted the title he said he had done so in order to give greater clout to his efforts to help the people of Brogieside. His wife was pleased to be Lady Miller and privately told her husband that there was a bit of the hypocrite in all of us!

The Lord Provost stepped forward. "Lord Miller of Brogieside", he began, "you have ignored all counsel, all advice and ultimately all orders from lawful authority. You have persisted with these activities and unauthorised constructions and defied the courts' bans on them. You have failed to demolish these buildings and other edifices which you constructed without municipal planning permission and have consistently utilised them for your illegal gatherings. What say you to these charges?"

Lord Miller gave his reply. "Our constructions and activities have done nothing to endanger anyone. I defy you to show me where even one life or one limb was lost in the execution of the many and varied projects here at Brogieside. In fact, our endeavours here have increased the life expectancy of all Brogieside residents, they have improved the health and general mental and physical well-being of the neighbourhood, they have provided them with employment, in short, they have made Brogieside a cleaner, safer and better place for all. Yet political neglect of this neighbourhood over the past 120 years has resulted in the deaths of thousands. Politicians past and present are guilty of murder on a grand scale. Not only have our hard work and industriousness not been the cause of death or injury, they have in fact saved and prolonged many a life. What say you to these civic improvements?"

Councilor Sandy Mackenzie Chairman of the city Planning Committee came up to Miller. "Aye, but they werena done through the proper legal and political channels", protested Mackenzie.

"And why should that matter?", interjected Lady Flora Miller. "What have you politicians ever done for Brogieside?"

"Aye but at least we're elected, you eens (ones) are no", said Councilor Mark Fiddlemore.

"And so much for your election pledges", said Lord Miller angrily.

"Who elected you?", demanded the Lord Provost.

"The residents here merely followed my example and my advice", replied Miller. "Does it embarrass you that the non-elected have succeeded in doing in two years what you politicians have failed to do in 120 years!"

"Enough of your impertinence", yelled the Lord Provost at Miller.

"Enough of your arrogance", yelled Miller back at him.

"Now once and for all", demanded the Lord Provost, "will you dissolve your associations, cease your projects and dismantle the buildings you illicitly erected?"

"Get lost", was all that Miller said in reply.

The Lord Provost looked at the Chief Constable and nodded. The Chief Constable looked at and nodded to another police officer who looked at and nodded to a sergeant, and the looking and the nodding continued all the way down to a line of police cars and bulldozers stationed on the perimeter of Brogieside. The police cars and the bulldozers started moving into the Brogieside. Dozens of police invaded the neighbourhood and before not too long Miller and his "chief cohorts" were in handcuffs. They looked on in horror as the bulldozers dashed to pieces all the work of the previous two years. An hour later, the community hall, the sports complex, the plots, the gardens, the 20 inch telescope and lecture hall were reduced to a pile of rubble. The canals were filled in with sand and earth and the plots and gardens were churned over and their vegetables uprooted. Cows, pigs, goats and sheep with nowhere to graze filled the now desolate streets with their mournful mooing, grunting and baaing. Not even the nuclear power plant had been spared. All the political talk about "saving the planet" and "protecting the environment" from nuclear power proved to be just that – political. For all the blah and hot air from politicians of all parties about the "dangers" of nuclear power, radioactive material was left lying willy nilly all over the area where the power plant had been. So it now dawned on the observers of this wanton destruction that radioactive material was only a threat to the environment under certain political conditions!! The Brogieside residents had put up quite a fight – and this time they felt that a bit of bottle - throating was perfectly justified. The members of the Brogieside resistance who were caught were herded into police vans and taken off to "the local nick".

"You miserable bastards" hollered Miller. "Brogieside could have been an example for many such neighbourhoods in Britain to follow. The whole nation would have benefited. Don't you have the wit to see that?"

"Aye noo, we see it", said Councilor Gordon Swickem", but we jist canna be haeing it. An that's a there is aboot it".

CHAPTER 8.

CLOSE ENCOUNTERS.

At his debriefing at NASA HQ in Florida, Terrence Brayson gave a full account of the past four years. He said absolutely nothing about the appalling scene he witnessed during his last moments on Mars. He was desperately hoping that the long awaited explanation would be forthcoming, but it never came and Brayson left the debriefing room a heartily disappointed man. The chairman of the senate Space Committee had concluded: "Now y'all understand that Mars is just a waste a space. Now we in this here committee don't see no reason to continue with explorin' it".

The chairman of the Congressional Finance Committee spoke up in similar vein: "Now I eh concur with ma colleague on this one. We ain't gonna be a recommendin' that any more money is given to this lil ol' Mars project thing. Yi see we all got a responsibility to the taxpayers and them thar other folks".

"Perhaps I should have asked about what I saw during those last moments on Mars?" thought Brayson admonishing himself. On second thoughts, he guessed he was right not to have mentioned it. Maybe they were testing him. "No", he concluded, "I was right to keep my mouth buttoned".

Outside the NASA complex, David Henderson was waiting for him.

"What will you do now?", Henderson asked Brayson.

"I don't know", replied Brayson. "I need time to take stock; to take stock not just of my professional life but of my personal life".

"What about the briefing Terry, how did that go?"

Terry instantly smelled a rat and the alarm bells of caution started to ring inside his head. "Be careful what you say?", his inner thoughts advised him. "This could be another test".

In answer to Henderson's query, Terry advised his colleague that he was not at liberty to relate the proceedings. "All I can say is that those questioning me were politicians. They consisted of the chairman of the Senate Space Committee and the chairman of the Congressional Finance Committee. Two other members of each committee were present apart from the chairmen. There was surprisingly only one NASA official present – and he was of relatively junior rank. And that's as much as I can say".

"Mmm I see, I see", muttered Henderson in reply. "Interesting!".

In view of the fact that Lord Stephen Miller had not engaged in any criminal activity during his "escapades" in Brogisdie, Glasgow Crown Court handed him down a lenient two year gaol sentence. Though Lady Flora had frequently visited her husband during his incarceration, they nevertheless had a lot to talk about when he was released after his two year stretch behind bars. Flora and her friends salvaged what they could from the wreckage, they quite literally picked up the pieces, and did what they could to make life tolerable in the Brogieside.

"Have you been keeping up your hospital rounds?", Stephen asked Flora.

"Yes I have", she replied.

"How is that amnesia lassie doing? The one we found

lying in the street a couple of years back. You remember her? It looked like a bottle - throating job."

"She recovered her senses and told us her name was Patricia Laister and that she was a journalist from the US who wanted to get info. for an article on Brogieside".

"Which publication did she work for?"

"Oh it was some sort of new magazine called *Cleaner and Better Cities*"

"I'd like to visit her. She could spread the Brogieside story far and wide".

"You'll no dae that Stephen. She discharged herself from hospital last month and we've no trace of her. She must have gone back to the States."

"That's a pity. She would have been great publicity for us."

At his home in Washington DC, Terry Brayson answered a ring on his doorbell. He was astonished to see Sheila Mitchell, David Henderson and Alexander Johnstone standing right there on his doorstep. All the memories of his last two days on Mars came flooding back. They were the first humans he had clapped eyes on for two years. Once safely inside Terry's home, they had this message for him. The NASA Administrator wants to see you.

"The Administrator!!", exclaimed Terry.

"Yep", said Johnstone. "The big boss himself. And he wants to see you next week."

"Your flight, pick up and hotel are all booked", added Sheila.

"This sounds real heavy duty", Terry said. "Any idea what it's about?"

"Yes, but....."

"....you can't tell me" said Terry anticipating Johnstone's reply.

Bernard Tristram, for all his high rank and burdensome responsibilities, was a fairly modest sort of man. He wasted very little time. After asking Brayson how he was, and after Brayson assuring him that he was fine, he said "there's someone here I would like you to meet. Just follow me into the adjoining room".

Brayson was beginning to feel bored already. "Some other tedious politician or NASA official", he thought to himself. When he entered the adjoining room, he beheld a sight which made his jaw drop and his eyes almost pop out of their sockets. This time he thought he really must be dreaming as he stood in paralysed fear and awe.

"Cynthia! Cynthia! Is it really you.?", he eventually managed to blurt out.

"Yes Terry darling. It's really me", she assured him.

And they fell into each other's arms in a passionate embrace of tears, hugs and kisses.

Terry and Cynthia looked at each other's tear drenched countenances. At last Terry said, "but how Cynthia, how? I, I mean the explosion, the failure of the oxygen supply, the destruction of the mother ship....I....I don't understand... I just, I just...don't get it."

"Have you heard of wormholes?", she asked him.

"Y Y Yes Yes" he stammered.

"The mother ship scraped the edge of one and its force field caused the ship's systems to malfunction. I managed to locate the main entrance to this, the Earth-Mars wormhole, and in a few seconds I was back on Earth. I crash landed, so to speak, in the Scottish city of Glasgow in one of its rougher neighbourhoods called Brogieside. I was amnesic for nearly two years but at last recovered my senses. In order not to reveal secrets, I passed myself off as a journalist under the name of Patricia Laister".

Terry was astonished. Oh but how so pleased he was to see Cynthia again.

"God really does work in mysterious ways", he said. "How truly sorry I am that I cursed God over your apparent loss".

"Well, we're only human," said Cynthia.

"Now we have a very serious proposition for you, Brayson", said the Administrator in solemn and serious tones.

"Which is?" asked Brayson with elevated voice.

"Would you like to go back to Mars and settle there permanently?" said the Administrator rather bluntly.

"No damned way", cried Brayson. "You must be joking. You must be out of your bloody mind".

"I want you to look at these pictures of Mars", said one of the NASA officials who was attending the meeting. "They really are most informative".

"I've been there", said Terry. "Who is anyone in this entire Universe to tell me about Mars? If anyone is going to do any 'informing' about Mars, then that person is going to be me", said Terry in very ill-humoured tones.

"Just look", said another NASA official rather calmly and totally unshaken by Terry's outburst.

When Terry looked at the screen, he saw before him not a bleak and desolate landscape but the most beautiful gardens and valleys he had ever seen. Trees, flowers, plants, shrubs, birds of gorgeous colours flew before him. Meadows full of horses, fields full of cattle and sheep, lakes full of the most exotic fish. It could have been anywhere on Earth.

"But I didn't see anything like this on Mars", cried Brayson. "Is this some sort of sick joke?"

"These 'greenified' areas of the planet are not to be made known", warned the Administrator.

"By the way, Cynthia", said Terry. "I'm sorry I kind of

cheated you out of being the first human to step on to Mars".

Cynthia laughed. "Oh Terry! I was born on Mars. There have been colonies of specially selected people there for the past 25 years".

"Then why was I left languishing on that damned awful base?", protested Terry.

"The plan was to discover which of you were the most suitable for living in our new Martian paradises", said the Administrator. "Of course, due to the awful accident, it never quite worked out that way. However, we observed all your actions and you passed with summa cum laud!"

"So"! exclaimed Terry loudly. "It wasn't my imagination after all!"

Everyone looked rather bemused. "What wasn't just your imagination Terry?" asked Cynthia.

"I.. I mean... I sometimes thought I saw vehicles on the horizon.... a forest in the distance... a house..!!" he stammered

"You imagined nothing", explained Cynthia. "We were watching you?"

"I really must say though that I did like the Christmas scenes", said Terry. "Now that really did cheer me up".

"What 'Christmas scenes'?" asked Cynthia somewhat bemused. "You were the one who put up these scenes on the base".

"I eh don't know what you mean Cynthia. I never had any Christmas scenes on the base. I never ever felt in a 'Christmassy mood' in that place."

The NASA Administrator and the other officials were as puzzled as Cynthia and Terry.

"Oh well, never mind" shrugged Terry.

"Whatever it was, it was quite spectacular", said Cynthia.

"Anyway, now I understand, now I'm in the picture", Terry explained, "but do Congress and the White House know about this Martian enterprise?"

"Like hell they do" said the Administrator.

"I've got an e-message from Patricia Laister", Flora told her husband.

"What does she want?" Stephen asked her.

"She wants us to come over to the States to work on a documentary on Brogieside", explained Flora. "All expenses paid".

"Let's waste no more time then", said Stephen.

A week later, Stephen and Flora were taken to NASA HQ where they were introduced to Terrence Brayson.

"This is a great privilege", said Stephen, "but what has this to do with the Brogieside documentary?"

"I also fail to see any connection", said Terry.

The Administrator, with a wry smile on his face, turned to Terry and asked, "do you know Professor Sean Miles?". He then turned to Stephen and asked "have you heard of Professor Ernest Gray?"

After all that he had been through, Terry Brayson was now far beyond being shocked. However, Stephen and Flora stood agape.

All was revealed to them. Little had they known that they had been conversing with a man on Mars.

"I'm so glad you're going to come with us", said Cynthia.

"Yes", said Terry. "We could certainly use a good radio electronics man on Mars".

"Within ten to fifteen years, most of Mars will be green", said the Administrator. "More people will be taken there to inhabit the planet. Yet, of all the things we have ferried to Mars, there are two things we just don't want there."

"And what would these be?" asked Stephen.

"Politics and politicians", answered the Administrator. "Now considering your experiences, I don't think you would quarrel with that."

"Well", mused Stephen, "I disagree. I think we should be charitable and big-hearted. I want them to be taken too."

"You do!!!" exclaimed the astonished Administrator.

"Yes" answered Stephen, "I want them taken to Pluto".

Everyone roared with laughter.

CONCLUSION.

Dear Dr. Fraser,

I am very happy that my predecessor made publicly available the true nature of the Mars missions of the earlier part of this century. Mars is now a truly beautiful planet and it gives me great pleasure to relate to you that Brogieside is a veritable paradise, a real Garden of Eden. It is the most beautiful of all of Mars' vast fields and open meadows.

You ask me what happened on the occasion of Terrence Brayson's departure from Mars just after he entered the rescue craft. As he took one last look at the base which he had worked so hard at making functional over the two years he had been stranded on Mars, the robots which he thought had become permanently non-functional suddenly started to move. The fifty mechanical monsters, as if by magic, suddenly came to life, and started moving towards the base. Of course, there was nothing at all magical in their movements; NASA had full and total control of them. Their systems had been designed to reject all local programming and control – that is why Brayson was unable to render them functional. The larger robotic machines with industrial, earth-moving and other such heavy duty capabilities, had had their demolition components activated and they proceeded at once in a frenzy of destruction. In less than twenty minutes, the base and all its facilities which Brayson had so lovingly cared for was reduced to a smouldering wreck – a Martian junk yard. And what most of all broke Brayson's heart was the death of his livestock. When these huge robotic machines smashed through the steel and glass of the pasture areas, all the animals suddenly became exposed to the -57C temperature, cosmic radiation and the highly toxic CO2 atmosphere of Mars and died within seconds.

Now the most obvious question is "why?". While NASA was justly proud of what they in general and Terrence Brayson in particular had achieved on Mars, the politicians were not quite so happy. They, rightly or wrongly, saw Brayson's accomplishments as a blueprint for an alternative political, economic and social order, one that essentially excluded politics, at least as it was currently understood and practiced. The White House, the CIA, the FBI, the Pentagon – in short, the whole political establishment, brought their entire collective muscle to weigh down on NASA which then had no choice but to "do the political needful". Glasgow City Council was regularly briefed by Washington about the radio messages between "Miles" and "Gray". It was just plain gall for the Glasgow authorities that the garbled and distorted messages between an unemployed radio hack in Brogieside and a stranded astronaut on a dead and barren planet had proved far superior to all the detailed and technical ideas of over a hundred years of City Planners in transforming the Brogiesdie neighbourhood. Brayson and Miller, alias Miles and Gray, had succeeded by default where meticulous planning had consistently failed.

Smarting from this severe blow, NASA redoubled its efforts with its hidden "Genesis Agenda". Over the years and decades Mars became greener and more people went there to colonise the planet .NASA and its agents on Mars stamped out anything which even began to smell of politics .

You ask me if Mars is still "politics free". Unfortunately not I regret to inform you. Various factions have arisen and have proven to be impossible to eliminate. All that NASA and its Martian administrators can now do is to contain and control it as best as possible. Such I suppose is human nature. Perhaps it was naïve to believe that Mars would remain forever a "politically free zone". Over the centuries utopias have been tried and have invariably failed. Those of us who are endowed with sufficient realism and a reasonable knowledge of the Classics, will recall Aristotle's most apt observation that "Man is a political animal." His travels, whether near or far, do not alter his nature; he will always remain a political animal. Wherever he goes, his nature goes with him.

Yet, there is something else in Man: it is a yearning for a long gone Golden Age. It is a harking back to the Garden of Eden, a quest to recover a paradise lost. But due to Man's fallen nature, his endeavours will produce politics rather than Paradise. He wishes for Paradise but his acts are political. It is somewhat reminiscent of chapter 7 of St. Paul's epistle to the Romans where the apostle treats upon the war between the spirit and the flesh. Concomitant with this battle is surely the one which is waged between Paradise and politics. No doubt, in the centuries to come, as Mankind spreads out into the Galaxy, the Genesis and Eden experiments will be tried repeatedly, but unless I am being unduly pessimistic, my prognosis is that Man's fallen nature will consistently dominate his finer spiritual strivings. In the opening years of this century, a BBC journalist by the name of John Simpson said that "every paradise has its worm". When we look back over the events of the past few decades and examine them in the light of other attempts at utopia, then sooner of later the inevitable worm is bound to make its debut from its hidey hole. The account of the events described by Sir Reginald Wosley bear this analysis out in both literal and figurative forms. The wormhole destroyed the mother ship carrying Brayson and his crew. Yet, it saved Cynthia Dobson. The chemical that Glasgow City Council ordered to be sprayed on the plots and gardens of Brogieside gave rise to a devouring worm that consumed all the fruit and vegetables that the people of Brogieside so cared for and tended during those two exciting years. There were the worms that demolished Brogieside and the "worms" that laid the Cerberus base on Mars in utter ruin.

What lesson can be learned from all of this? Are we to dismiss it as the hopes of starry-eyed dreamers? I would ring out a resounding "no" in answer to these two questions. And why? It is because tremendous practical hard work and passionate drive went into the high ideals which motivated the pioneers of Brogieside and Cerberus. While these, and other utopian enterprises, do have the great potential of letting us glimpse through their fleeting existence to the fact that Man does harbour within himself the realisation of what the perfect society ought to be like, we still keep before us the pragmatic understanding that there can never be another Eden, at least not this side of eternity.

And then there is the strange phenomenon of "the manger" formation seen in distant rocks. Like so many phenomena on Mars, these cannot be explained away as being mere tricks of light and shadow. They appear every December 25th at various locations on the planet and all consist of identical life-size figures of the Holy Family and the stable animals. When viewed through telescopic lenses, the figures instantly reveal mere rock formations; the same thing happens when expeditions are made to these nativity scenes. And if you thought, Dr. Fraser, that that is strange, there is yet more. The same phenomena present themselves on December 25th among the ruined heaps and rubble of Brogieside in Glasgow. What it all means is something we must judge for ourselves. My own take on the matter, for whatever it may be worth, is

that building utopias which exclude the Prince of Peace, can be nothing more than a futile undertaking.
   Sir Giles Henry Paterson.
   (Astronomer Royal)
   2081.

—ONLY HALF BELIEVE WHAT YOU SEE—

Chapter 1.

I can't get away to marry you to-day, my wife won't let me.

"Pig"! screamed Sylvia Carson as she gave her husband Harold Carson an almighty slap across the side his face, and she screamed the same compliment again as she administered a slap to his other cheek. "Here we are, only three months into our marriage and you're already flirting with fancy women. You two-timing swine", Sylvia accused her husband.

"Calm yourself down Sylvia. You really shouldn't get so hysterical. You won't do your blood pressure any good".

"I don't know what kind of a household our children are coming into", sobbed Sylvia, "but you are certainly no example for their future moral development. And to think that we go to church every Sunday and are thought of as a model couple in Free Methodist circles. It is so pretentious and hypocritical".

"Look Sylvia", pleaded her husband, "if you'd only let me get a word in edge I could explain everything".

"Huh! You mean explain away everything", said Sylvia.

Harold took a deep breath and managed to compose himself. "As you know Sylvia", he began, "I've been engaged in some pretty top secret work at the Home Office's laboratories here in London. Rita is part of that research and I'm not at liberty to say anything more. I'm not having an affair as you so hysterically imagine, I'm just simply performing my occupational duties as a bio-engineer."

"And is taking her about in your car and constantly touching at her and even looking deeply into her eyes part of your eh ha ha 'occupational duties'", said Sylvia in mock laughter while making the inverted commas sign with her fingers for "occupational duties".

"Yes!", said Harold firmly in reply.

"Get out of this house, get out get out!!", screamed Sylvia. "I don't ever want to see you again! You think because I'm a simple teacher of French and not a high falutin research scientist that I don't know anything. Extra time at the laboratories in the evening - indeed! You think I'd fall for that one. I've been watching you and your Rita for weeks".

"Excuse me Dr. Carson", said a young brunette secretary who called at Harold's office, "the Research Director would like to see you".

Dr. Nathanial Armitage , the Research Director, was not the type of man to waste time on small talk and friendly chit chat. Every minute of his time had to be accounted for and not a second was to be wasted. Not forgetting these personality traits in his boss, Carson knew that there was something important brewing. He had no idea what it could be about, but it was certainly not an invitation for a morning cuppa and a digestive biscuit!

"Come in Harold", was the reply to Carson's knock on the RD's office door. "Do have a seat", said the RD as he beckoned Carson to a chair in front of his large mahogany desk.

"How are things with you, Harold?" asked the RD.

"Well, eh, fine" replied Carson.

"Your work, your research, the experiments all fine?", continued the RD in enquiring mode.

"Fine, fine, eh no problems at all", answered Carson as he wondered what all this was leading up to.

"Are you sure?", the RD pressed him.

"Nathanial", said Carson, "there's something amiss, isn't there? Could you please come to the point?"

"You've been looking rather down in the mouth recently, Harold", replied Armitage.

"I know you're a very busy man, Nathanial. This will take some time to explain".

"You're separated from your wife, aren't you Carson?", said the RD rather bluntly.

"Well, doesn't my change of address sort of tell you that?", Carson bleated rather sadly.

"It's about Rita, isn't it?", suggested the RD.

"How on Earth do you know that?", gasped Carson

"Oh Harold", sighed Armitage, "I wasn't exactly born yesterday, you know. Rumour was bound to get around. Sylvia had just got to find out sooner or later." Armitage then stared fixedly and silently at Carson.

"You didn't tell her anything, did you Harold. You kept that bloody mouth of yours shut, didn't you?" growled the RD.

"My being a Christian man constrains me from replying to you in the way that I feel like doing", said Carson, whose blood pressure was now soaring. "Of course I didn't, you silly man. Had I done so, do you think I'd be living in cheap rented accommodation in Stockwell rather than in my beautiful home at Hampstead Heath?"

"I don't share your convictions Carson," said Armitage, "but your integrity and honesty are above question and I'm sure this stems from your religious beliefs and practices".

"Well, thank you, Armitage", relied Carson rather tersely, "but I don't see what the point of all this is or where it is leading to?"

Without saying anything further, Armitage picked up the phone on his desk. "Hello, laboratory", he said, "get Rita out, I'm coming down". He glanced over at Carson and said "come on!"

Armitage and Carson took a lift to the laboratories which were located deep under ground.

"Just what is all this about", demanded Carson.

"I'm trying to help you", said Armitage.

"I fail to see how", muttered Carson.

"You'll see, trust me", Armitage assured him.

Chapter 2.

Is this a dagger I see before me?

Armitage, Carson, and Rita were alone in a small adjoining room. Armitage opened a metallic cupboard and took out a syringe.

"Administer this to Rita please Harold", said Armitage quite non chalant.

"Eh, what is this, what's eh going on?" asked a rather flummoxed Harold Carson.

"Just do exactly as I say", said Armitage slowly, ploddingly and calmly.

Carson looked at Armitage and then at Rita. Armitage looked at Carson and then at Rita.

"Go on!", said Armitage.

Carson emptied the contents of the needle into Rita's arm. In less than a minute she was dead.

Mrs. Sylvia Carson answered a ring at her front door later that morning.

"And what the hell do you want?", said Sylvia sternly to Harold who stood there rather sheepishly on the doorstep.

"Come down to the laboratories and all will be revealed", answered her estranged husband.

"Humph", muttered Sylvia. "I don't see what there is to explain."

"Sylvia, don't be so obstinate. At least, at the very least, give me a chance", pleaded Harold.

Harold and Sylvia drove to the laboratories in frosty silence. They took the lift to the main research area under ground and proceeded to the little room where Rita, just a few hours before, had been administered a lethal dose. Armitage was there, standing over the body of Rita which now lay on a kind of operating table.

Sylvia gave out a slight shriek when she saw the cadaver stretched out on the table.

"Do you recognize the woman lying over there?", asked her husband

"It's...it's eh eh R R Rita, is is isn't it", stammered Sylvia in response.

"Correct", was all that Harold answered.

"But...but wh what happened?" asked the shocked Sylvia.

Carson looked at Armitage. Armitage looked back at Carson and simply said "tell her".

"I murdered her", said Carson quite calmly, and picking up the empty syringe continued "I administered to her this lethal dose".

Sylvia put her hands to her face in horror. "Oh my God, oh my God, I I I didn't ask for murder. Oh God! Who are you? What are you? Have I married some psychopathic killer as well as a womaniser? Is this some sort of Bluebeard's den?"

"Be quiet Sylvia", commanded her husband. "Now you will have to be witness to the autopsy".

Sylvia shrunk back in a fit of horror as Armitage made the first incision with a scalpel along the femur of Rita's right leg. Sylvia wanted to dash out of the room but Harold physically prevented her. He shook her, slapped her face and told her to watch carefully at Dr. Armitage's autopsy.

At first there appeared to be nothing unusual. Skin, fat and muscle tissue were pealed away – however, no blood appeared during the cutting. What did eventually appear made Sylvia petrified with fear. Instead of the skeletal structure that would normally be revealed in the course of such a medical procedure, long metal rods connected to each other ran all the way down Rita's leg. When the entire cadaver had been dissected, a complete metallic skeleton could be seen.

Rita's head was the most interesting of all. It did not contain anything that could be described as a brain; what was inside of Rita's head looked to Sylvia like a cross between neural tissue and the inside of a computer's hard drive.

At the end of the autopsy, Sylvia just stood gaping in awe before fainting into Harold's arms.

When Sylvia came round, Harold was fanning her with some office paper and holding a stiff brandy in front of her. She looked over to the operating table to see some laboratory technicians clearing the last of Rita away.

Upstairs in the RD's office, Sylvia and Harold sat in front of Armitage.

The RD proceeded in tones which could be described as a cross between reverential solemnity and more than subtle hints of threats. "What you have seen Sylvia is most top secret and classified. You must speak of it to no-one. You must never, never, never discuss this matter with anyone. What you saw, you did not see! What you heard, you did not hear! Where you have been, you have not been! Do I make myself perfectly and abundantly clear?"

"Yes of course", said Sylvia. "My lips are sealed. I will breathe not a word of this to a single soul". Turning to her husband she said with tear filled eyes "Oh Har darling! I'm sorry. I'm so sorry. I was so wrong, so utterly wrong about you". And she fell into his arms sobbing and crying her heart out. "Please forgive me, please forgive me", she pleaded.

"Of course I do darling, of course I do", he assured her. "How could you have possibly known?"

"I'm sorry about the distress this has caused you Sylvia", said Armitage now speaking in apologetic tones, "but this was the only way we could convince you of your husband's fidelity."

"Thank you Dr. Armitage", replied Sylvia. "I'm indebted to you".

"I know you're not a scientist Sylvia", said the RD, "but I know you are an intelligent lady and have seen that Rita was a robot".

"Yes of course", said Sylvia.

"My touching and feeling of Rita and my looking into her eyes was purely for inspectional and checking purposes", Harold explained. "When I was taking her out I was checking her maneuverability and navigational systems. We hope to have perfected this technology in two years time - by 2027".

"Oh before that", said Armitage. "We hope by the end of this year".

"We are in the process of developing a new branch of science called 'robiology'", Armitage explained to her. "It is a combination of conventional computer technology, robotics and genetics. Information is increasing in such leaps and bounds, especially in the sciences, that we are simply running out of storage capacity. Magnetic tape and silicon chips are easily degradable. However, the genome can contain millions of times more information than silicon chips and last for hundreds of thousands of years. Also, it can be reproduced. So when a person dies, his or her knowledge does not necessarily have to die."

"So are we talking about clones?", Sylvia asked.

"Only in terms of genetics, but not in the science fiction sense of the entire personality of an individual", explained Armitage. "A person's knowledge in the form of memory taken from imprints of the frontal cortex, the parietal cortex, the anterior cingulate and the basal ganglia are fed into synthetic neural DNA. When wired up to a computer, the robot can calculate or give advice based on its experience."

"But you've destroyed Rita", said Sylvia.

"We've got a cupboard full of Ritas", laughed Armitage. "We sacrificed one for the demonstration you saw".

"May I ask who the real Rita is?", enquired Sylvia.

Armitage looked sad for a moment. "Rita was a brilliant nuclear scientist. She was working with the Ministry of Defence on atomic bomb research. She died of Multiple Sclerosis last year. Rita was…. she was, she was my wife".

CHAPTER 3.

NOW YOU SEE ME, NOW YOU DON'T.

Carson took his wife back to their home at Hampstead and then drove back to his place of work at the Home Office laboratories. A sense of satisfaction and relief came over him. His marriage was back on tracks and he felt that a brilliant career lay before him.

One evening, a few weeks later, when at around 5pm Harold Carson came home, he called out for his wife. "Hi honey, I'm home". But there was no reply. "Honey, hi... honey". He searched all the rooms but could see no sign of her. "Maybe she's gone down to the grocer's", thought Harold. The evening dragged on but Sylvia did not show up. Harold called her on her mobile – but no answer. Later, he rang her parents' home and the homes of her siblings but he had no joy there either. Harold now began to get worried. He thought of calling the police but decided to leave things for another day. "Perhaps she's in one of her moods", he conjectured.

At work, Harold tried her mobile number numerous times but with the same message "the number you have dialed is currently unavailable". He wanted to speak to Armitage about it, but he felt that he had bothered the RD enough with personal matters. When Carson drove home that evening, it was the same cold and silent house that greeted him.

"That does it", he said, "I'm calling the police".

As he was about to pick up the 'phone and dial 999, there was a ring on the doorbell.

"Sylvia, Sylvia", he thought. However, it was just wishful thinking. Standing on the threshold was The Rev'd. Mr. Arnold Stacks the minister of the Hampstead Free Methodist Church which Harold and Sylvia attended. Another man, who was accompanying Mr. Stacks, was unknown to Harold.

After Harold had invited both gentlemen into his home, Mr. Stacks introduced The Rev'd Mr. Archibald Hammer to him. Mr. Hammer was Chief Minister of the Dorset United Brethren. The DUB was a recently formed eschatological sect which believed that the end of the world was only a few short years away. The three men spent at least four hours in conversation. At the beginning of their long session, Harold told the two clerics about Sylvia's disappearance.

"I think Dr. Armitage may know something about it", said Stacks.

"What! You know my boss", said Harold astonished.

"We know about him", said Hammer. "And we know all about the biological robots".

Carson just stared in utter shock.

Eventually Carson found his voice. "How d d ddo yyy you know about th th this?", he spluttered.

"We have DUB plants in the Home Office laboratories", explained Hammer.

"So we know about the the eh ... 'murder' of Rita and the autopsy", added Stacks.

"Well, and I thought the research station had 100% security", said Carson.

Hammer threw back his head in laughter. "There is no such a thing as 100% security", he roared.

"But what has all this to do with Sylvia", screamed Carson. "I want my wife back, is she safe, is she...is she... alive or dead".

"We honestly don't know" said Stacks. "However, there could be a connection. What exactly that connection is we just don't know, at least not at this stage."

"We'll do our best to find out and report back any information we get to you", Hammer assured him.

"You know the reason for the ongoing research into robiolgy, don't you Harold?", asked Stacks.

"Of course I do", answered Carson rather haughtily. "I'm a senior researcher at the laboratories and have played and continue to play a major role in the development of this new science".

"Obviously you're not senior enough", continued Stacks.

"If you were, you'd know the true object of the research", said Hammer.

"The object of the research is quite clear", said Carson. "It is to effect the massive enhancement of information storage capacity by combining the sciences of computers, robotics, genetics and neurology."

Stacks and Hammer looked at each other and then back at Carson with pitying smiles. The expressions on their faces seemed to convey the subliminal message "the poor boy's an innocent, the lad's naïve".

"Armitage and his inner circle have a hidden agenda", said Hammer.

"Their plan is to use these biological robots to take over the world", added Stacks.

"Either you are both mad or you must have me down as a real simpleton", laughed Carson.

"Look Harold", said Stacks. "We have not been reading too much science fiction, nor are we insulting your intelligence. Mr. Hammer has his spies in the laboratories and he has managed to get his hands on some top secret information".

"Yes, yes", sighed Carson. "And uh ha ha where is this secret information now?"

"Right here", said Hammer. The DUB parson opened a briefcase and handed Carson a sheet of paper.

"Read it now Harold, and read it carefully", Stacks advised him.

MEMORANDUM.
To: Dr. Nathanial Armitage
From: Dr. Timothy Green
Date: 23rd January 2025
Subject: Virus.

Your secret instructions have now been implemented. The robots have been infected with both computer and biological viri. When the robots have been strategically placed in the designated locations around the world, their biological viri will be released. This should create the influenza epidemic which should kill the weakest and most useless of humans.

Our plans for Operation Computer Crash are almost ready. When we feed in the information stored in the robotic synthetic DNA into the World Wide Web the entire WWW will collapse. We can then proceed apace militarily.

※　　※　　※

"I'd be naïve and simple if I believed the authenticity of this", objected Carson. "How could you possibly have had access to such classified information?"

"We know how to observe and exploit people's weaknesses", Hammer explained. "Nathanial Armitage has a weakness for beautiful young women".

"He eyes up Rachel May", said Stacks. "He thinks she doesn't know, but she does".

"Rachel May?", queried Carson. "Oh yes the brunette. One of the secretarial staff".

"He trusts her so much that he even leaves her alone in his office", said Hammer. "But she's one of our plants. The little cross which she wears around her neck is actually a flash drive. She has copied all of Armitage's files"

"We have a copy of them all on this flash drive right here" said Stacks. "Let's go to your desktop".

On his computer monitor, Carson saw many files and memos which he had seen before. Many documents came up on the screen which he himself had written. Others appeared which had come from Armitage to him.

"If you're still not totally convinced, you will be tomorrow morning!" said Stacks.

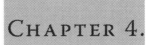

CHAPTER 4.

THE TWO REVERENDS.

The following morning, Harold Carson turned up at 9am as usual at the research laboratories. He was in a determined mood and was going to have it out with Armitage. While heading towards the RD's office, he cautioned himself to be firm yet polite with his boss. Soon he was outside Armitage's door and knocked.

"Come in", said a voice. Carson entered the office.

Armitage was sitting on a swivel chair facing towards the wall behind his desk.

"I know you're a very busy man Nathanial", said Carson, "but I really must talk to you."

Armitage swiftly wheeled round. He stared straight towards Carson.

"I want to talk about my wife, she's missing", said Carson.

Armitage continued to stare. "Wife. Rita, My.....missing".

Carson gingerly stepped forward to Armitage's desk. Armitage kept on staring blankly ahead. "Wife my Rita missing is", was all he could say.

In a fit of fury and frustration, Carson took Armitage by the lapels, pulled him out of his chair and threw him on the ground. There was a clank of metal as Armitage hit the ground. As he lay there, his incoherency became worse:

"malfunction, malfunction, wife, malfunction, missing, malfunction".

"It's obvious now that this is a robiological version of Nathanial Armitage", said a voice behind Carson.

Carson turned round and was shocked to find Arnold Stacks standing right behind him.

"What the hell is going on here?", "tell me or I'll smash your damned face in", threatened Carson.

"Smashing my damned face in will not advance by one iota your knowledge of what the hell is going on here", warned Stacks in a perfectly tranquil tone. "Just keep calm and follow me down to the laboratories". He then called out – "Rachel, will you please lock this office door and ensure that no-one enters".

"Yes of course Mr. Stacks", said the gorgeous brunette.

The laboratories were completely deserted.

"Where is everyone?" demanded Carson.

"Armitage told them to take the day off as the labs were to be given a security run over", replied Stacks.

"And why would he do that?", asked Carson.

"Because we kidnapped him and forced him to do so?" said Archibald Hammer emerging from behind a large piece of machinery.

"I thought you'd be around", said Carson quite calmly.

"We'll show you ample proof of Armitage's plans to conquer the world", said Hammer.

"You're a pair of madmen", said Carson gritting his teeth.

"Everything is now ready", a voice called out.

"All may come out now", shouted Stacks.

From behind cupboards and machinery and from under desks, seven masked men emerged..

"Who are they?", demanded Carson.

"All respected members of the Dorset United Brethren –

and – employees of HM Government", said Hammer as he left the laboratory.

"In other words, they're your spies and plants in the research laboratories", said Carson.

"If you like", said Stacks.

"Now ready Mr. Stacks" said one of the masked men who then handed Stacks a remote control device. Stacks pressed a button and at once the walls of the laboratory started to open up. Carson was flabbergasted. These were compartments he had never known about before. What flabbergasted him even more was what he saw behind these walls. All around the perimeter of the laboratory were stacked 30 nuclear warheads.

"Is the picture becoming clearer?", asked Stacks. "Is the message getting through to you at last as to what Armitage is up to?"

Before he could answer about twenty men armed with sub machine guns emerged from behind the warheads. Carson simply did not have the time to take in the fast moving events. In a few short seconds he was grabbed from behind and a chloroform soaked cloth was held firmly over his mouth and nose.

CHAPTER 5.

HIGH IN THE MISTY HIGHLANDS.

When Carson woke up his right arm was stinging. He must have been given a very powerful soporific after the initial dose of chloroform. He had no idea where he was. All he could hear was a low droning sound. Was it his head reeling from the effects of the drug? As he staggered to his feet he looked out of a porthole of a window and saw nothing but cloud. Now he realised that he was on a small jet plane. On the plane with him were six heavily armed guards.

"Where are we?", he asked one of them.

"Approaching Ben Nevis in Scotland" was the reply.

The plane, a modern wingless, vertical takeoff type and atomic powered, hovered over the top of the great mountain for about five minutes. A conversation between the pilot and ground control ensued for a few minutes. As he looked down below, Carson could see a part of the mountain open up. The plane descended into it.

The armed guards took Carson out of the plane, told him not to ask any questions, but that all would eventually be revealed to him. The guards took Carson to his living quarters where he was informed that he would find ample provisions and that he should be ready by eight o'clock the following morning to meet the Base Administrator.

"Did you have a good sleep?", asked the Base Administrator.

" I sort of had a sneaking feeling it would be you?", said Carson. "So, don't be surprised that I'm not surprised".

"I'm not", answered Stacks. "But there will be many more surprises for you yet, I assure you".

"Hmmph. You mean that Archibald Hammer is going to emerge from behind a panel or out of that picture of Bonnie Prince Charlie?"

"No, No, you won't be seeing Hammer", said Stacks.

"Just who are you and who do you work for?", demanded Carson.

Stacks slowly got up out of his chair. He walked over to an adjoining room and beckoned Carson to enter. Stacks put his finger to his mouth and then opened his mouth, put his tongue between his teeth and bit it. This was a clear message to Carson not to say a word. He took some sort of electronic device from his pocket and moved it around the room. After a few seconds he spoke. "Good, I think there are no bugs here".

Stacks then removed a tiny device from behind his upper teeth. "There now", he said.

The voice started to sound familiar. Stacks then put his hands behind his head and started fumbling around. A mask started to come away slowly but surely from Stack's face. Carson watched in awe struck wonder.

"Nathanial Armitage!", he bellowed out.

"Shoosh", he cautioned . You're the only one here who knows my real identity. There may be DUB plants here too. If there are any, they must feel confident in thinking that the real Stacks has infiltrated the base".

"Where is Sylvia?", demanded Carson.

"She's all right", Armitage assured him. "Trust me. I can't say any more at this stage".

"I take it you know what happened in London this morning", Carson asked.

"Absolutely everything", replied Armitage.

"And eh, your plan to hmmm – take over the world", said Carson.

"I don't think you ever seriously believed that, did you?", asked Armitage.

"No, but there is nevertheless more to all of this than meets the eye", said Carson. "There is no doubt some secret agenda is being played out somehow."

"In that you are right", said Armitage. "Be patient please Harold, be patient. All will unfold in due course. This evening you will see something that will bowl you over. It is however part of a piece in the jig-saw which will soon present you with the complete picture".

CHAPTER 6.

IT'S A BRAW, BRECHT, MEENLECHT, NECHT, THE NECHT.

The following midnight, Armitage (alias Stacks) and Carson drove to a lonely spot near a small lake about ten miles from the base. The area was cordoned off by the military. Armitage removed the "Stacks face" and "Stacks Voice". He gave Carson an identification card. "Here, show this at the checkpoint", he said.

After driving for about another mile, the car stopped. A few hundred yards away was a massive object in the shape of a flying saucer.

"Good Lord! Is this a UFO or what?!", exclaimed Carson.

"Well eh, yes", answered Armitage, "but not in the popular sense of the term".

Armitage led Carson to an office on the complex. Inside the office was a man busily looking over some technical papers.

"Thank you so much for coming, Sir Charles", said Armitage to the man. Then turning to Carson he said, "Harold, this is Sir Charles MacDouglas the Astronomer Royal for Scotland. Sir Charles, this is Dr. Harold Carson".

"I'm so pleased to meet you", said the Astronomer Royal. "Nathanial has told me all about you. I know you must feel rather angry about what has happened to you, but you will soon understand that there really was no other way."

"I know that something very unusual is going on", replied Carson.

"Harold, I would like you to watch some footage of the building of the craft you have just seen", said Armitage.

"But it must have taken years to build such a monster of a thing", said Carson.

"Just look at this", replied Armitage as he flicked a switch and some paneling on the wall parted to reveal a screen.

The footage showed hundreds of biological robots walking towards the site where the craft now stood.

"So I take it the robots assembled the flying saucer", conjectured Carson.

"Yyyes eh you could say that", answered the AR rather hesitatingly.

The three men watched the recording and saw the robots starting to arrange themselves in a circle. They also stood one on top of the other to a height of over 50 feet. The robots then began to weld themselves together.

"My God!", exclaimed Carson. "The robots *are* the flying saucer".

"Obviously", said Armitage.

"Now then", continued Armitage. "I want to show the part of the DVD where the robots are walking towards the assembly area, but this time in close up".

Many of the biological robots which Carson saw walking to their assembly area looked familiar. They were nuclear scientists, astronauts, astronomers and astro-physicists. However, there was one robot which Carson saw which made him jump out of his chair.

"Sylvia", he shouted.

"It's only a robotic version of her", Armitage assured him.

"But why? Why?", screamed Carson. "What do you want her brain patterns for? She's a languages teacher, not a scientist."

"Intelligence has uncovered a plot by the French authorities to sabotage this operation", the AR explained. "We want her knowledge of French to countermand any viral programming the French may have been able to put into the command and control system".

"You know how the French have constantly tried to undermine our defence capabilities?" said Armitage.

"Yes, of course", replied Carson. "But where is Sylvia now?"

"At the Ben Nevis Base", said Armitage. Carson breathed a sigh of relief.

"Now let's step outside and see the launch", the AR suggested.

The three men stood and watched the saucer slowly ascend into the air. By the time it was about three hundred feet in the air, it suddenly increased its speed and in a few split seconds was out of sight.

"It will reach its destination in about a week", said the AR.

"Now then" said Carson. "Perhaps you wouldn't mind explaining to me what all this is about".

"Let's go back inside", suggested the AR.

Once inside, the three men sat down at the large conference table. Armitage checked the place for bugging devices and shuttered the windows.

"This in fact is the second such saucer to be launched", said Armitage.

"The first one reached its destination a week ago and successfully completed its mission", added the AR.

"Please tell me exactly what you are talking about" Carson asked him.

"Have you heard of Asteroid Zenta?", the Astronomer Royal asked him.

"Yes", answered Carson.

"And have you heard that there was always a chance that it would collide with the Earth?", asked the AR.

"Yes, there are in fact many asteroids which cross Earth's orbit and have been considered as candidates for collision", said Carson.

"For the past five years , meticulous calculations have shown that in 2027, Asteroid Zenta would directly strike the Earth", said the AR.

"I don't see where all this is leading", said Carson.

"Please bear with us", said Armitage.

"I take it you know what the consequences would be for this planet if it came into collision with a half mile diameter asteroid", asked the AR.

"A disaster of truly global proportions", answered Carson.

"It would throw up reflecting dust particles into the atmosphere and cause another ice age", said the AR. "Sunlight reaching Earth would be reflected back into space by these particles in the stratosphere".

"What has the saucer and the robots got to do with this?", asked Carson.

"One of the robots on the first saucer had a camera which relayed pictures back to Earth", said Armitage. "Look at this footage".

The viewing screen displayed a flying saucer hovering over an asteroid.

"That's Asteroid Zenta", said Armitage.

The robots which actually made up the craft then

separated and descended on to the asteroid. They were spaced out at regular intervals across the asteroid.

"Now watch this", said Armitage.

All at once there was an almighty explosion – and the asteroid was no more.

"Do you get the picture now?" asked Armitage.

"Yes of course", answered Carson.

"A nuclear warhead was attached to each robot – the ones you saw in the laboratory in London when you were accosted by Stacks and Hammer", said Armitage.

"The robots were composed of the neurological DNA of astronomers and astronauts so that the composite craft could be successfully guided to the asteroid", said the Astronomer Royal. "The DNA of nuclear scientists was used to control and synchronise the explosion".

"But even after successfully blowing up the asteroid, there could still be large enough pieces of debris to cause a global disaster were they to hit the Earth", said Carson.

"That's why the second craft is on its way to the vicinity of the explosion just over two million miles away", explained Armitage. "It's mission is to make a survey of the vicinity and identify rocks which are over 100 feet in diameter. A robot with a nuclear warhead will then be dispatched to it to eliminate it."

"And if there are more such pieces of debris than robots?", asked Carson.

"We'll employ the same technique again", said the Astronomer Royal.

"And what has all this got to do with kidnapping Sylvia, and the Stacks and Hammer business?" Carson demanded.

"We'll explain that back at the Ben Nevis base", Armitage told him.

CHAPTER 7.

THINGS AREN'T ALWAYS
WHAT THEY SEEM.

Back in Armitage's office at the Base, the Research Director and the Astronomer Royal continued their explanation of the events of the past few days.

"We knew exactly what Stacks and Hammer were planning", said Armitage.

"How did you know?", Carson asked him.

"From Rachel of course", he explained.

"So she was a kind of double agent – but really working for you?" Carson asked.

"Yes", replied Armitage.

"And how can you be so sure?" continued Carson.

"She infiltrated the DUB by posing as one of Hammer's flock", said Armitage.

"Can you really be so sure?", Carson pressed him.

Armitage took a deep breath. "Rachel is my daughter".

"We wanted Stacks and Hammer to continue with their plan which was to kidnap you and force you to sabotage the operation", Sir Charles MacDouglas explained.

"Why?", Carson asked him.

"So that we could find out exactly who the DUB plants were", said Armitage. "The men who rushed out on you from behind the nuclear war-heads in the laboratories were not Stacks' and Hammer's ones, they were from MI5. They arrested Stacks and the seven masked men immediately".

"And Hammer?" enquired Carson.

"As he had left the laboratory just before the MI5 men acted, he managed to elude us", said Armitage.

"According to Stacks and Hammer, you had been kidnapped", said Carson.

"Oh I was. But we had to let their plan continue so that we could find out as much as possible", Armitage explained to him. "I was wearing a homing device, so it was easy for other MI5 agents to track me down to a crypt in Stacks' church where some other terrorists were guarding me".

"And then?", asked Carson.

"Dressed in one of the terrorist's outfits, we proceeded to the base. I passed through unrecognised. When I got down to the labs a face mask of Stacks using his DNA and computerised photography was ready for me. We also made a device based on his vocal chord DNA so that I could mimic his speech. Dressed as Stacks I got out of the base and proceeded here with you".

"I didn't see you on the plane", said Carson

"As I was wearing a helmet and in co-pilot's uniform, you wouldn't have done so", explained Armitage.

"Why did you come to this base as The Reverend Stacks? Why not as Dr. Nathanial Armitage?", Carson wanted to know.

"If this base is also DUB penetrated", said Armitage, "then it's safer for me to come here in this guise".

"Why did you have to kidnap Sylvia?", asked Carson rather sternly. "Why not simply ask both of us about using her neurological DNA?"

"Both for her protection and security reasons", Armitage told him.

"So Stacks and Hammer thought you planned to take over the world with robiology technology?", asked Carson.

"Hammer knew all about the asteroid. His DUB had got hold of leaked information from the Royal Observatory in Edinburgh. He so desperately wanted the asteroid to impact with the Earth".

"Whyever?", asked an astonished Carson.

"It was his big chance to prove his apocalyptic doctrines as being true", said Armitage. "He identified this asteroid as the star 'wormwood' in the Book of Apocalypse'. In Chapter 8 this object is described as a star which falls on the Earth. 'And the third part of those creatures died, which had life in the sea, and the third part of the ships was destroyed. And the third angel sounded the trumpet, and a great star fell from heaven, burning as it were a torch, and it fell on the third part of the rivers, and upon the fountains of waters: And the name of the star is called Wormwood. And the third part of the waters became wormwood; and many men died of the waters, because they were made bitter'. So we know all about this lunatic".

"Can I see Sylvia now?", Carson asked.

"No – not quite yet", said Armitage. "There are still some more vital things to be done first".

"How far up officialdom does this knowledge go?", asked Carson.

"Very few people indeed", replied Armitage. "The monarch, the PM, the Home Secretary, the Foreign Secretary, the Defence Secretary and a handful of senior civil servants and top military brass".

"I wonder why Hammer did not wait for you and make his way here to the base", said Carson.

"Perhaps he had other plans", conjectured Armitage.

"Maybe he smelled a rat when Stacks delayed his coming from the labs. We can only guess."

"Why guess when we can ask Hammer himself?", said Carson.

"What on Earth do you mean?", asked a rather puzzled Armitage.

Carson then pounced on the Astronomer Royal and after a bit of a tussle, pulled a revolver from out of his inside jacket pocket.

"You can take off the mask now Mr. Hammer", said Carson.

"I I I dddon't know what you're talking about", the AR protested.

Pointing the revolver at his head Carson simply said: "I'll count to ten. One.."

Slowly and reluctantly the mask was taken off and it revealed the face of Archibald Hammer.

"Good Heavens!", exclaimed Armitage. You're a genius Harold. But...but ... how did you know?"

"The Astronomer Royal for Scotland is a shorter and stockier man than Hammer", explained. Carson. "I used to attend his lectures when I visited Scotland. I'm a keen amateur astronomer."

"Then let's get him in handcuffs and placed under arrest", said Armitage.

"Not until you've taken off *your* mask ...eh... Dr. Armitage. Or should I say ...Mr. Stacks?"

"What – you're mad Carson. You're crazy" yelled Armitage.

"I'll give you ten seconds as well" said Carson calmly and slowly.

Armitage's mask was peeled away to reveal the face of Arnold Stacks.

"Wearing a double mask Stacks – just as I thought", said Carson. "You think I'd fall for that cock and bull story? Now where is the real Dr. Armitage?"

Stacks sighed. "Being held prisoner in a crypt in my church".

"I'll get MI5 straight away" Carson said. Carson told the Intelligence Service where exactly Dr. Armitage was located. "And arrange for the military police to enter Ben Nevis Base".

"How did you know it was me Carson?", asked a rather dejected Stacks.

"If this was Hammer it was obvious that you were Stacks. Also, I remember your telling me in the office in London that you were not of my persuasion. Armitage simply never talks religion. That is not the sort of thing he would say. I smelled a rat right away. And then there was your long and accurate quote from the Apocalypse. To the best of my knowledge, Armitage has never darkened a church door in his life; he is an atheist from an atheist family. There is no way that he could have made such a long winded and accurate biblical quote."

The expression on Armitage's face was as if to say: "why did I make such a stupid mistake?"

"Now then", continued Carson. "Why did you bring me here? What exactly is your game?"

Stacks and Hammer just looked down at the floor and remained silent.

"You damn well speak up", yelled Carson, "or I'll kill both of you here and now – and I'm not bluffing". And he pushed the nozzle of the gun into Stacks' head and pulled back the safety catch.

"All right, all right", cried Stacks, "just take that thing out of my head. When we heard that the asteroid had been destroyed, we thought that the next best thing would be to bring back a couple of these war heads and have them fall on to the Earth; one in the Kalahari Desert and another in the Pacific Ocean. That way we'd make some kind of an apocalyptic point while minimising casualties. Your job was to change the co-ordinates on two of the robots so that they would return to Earth. We were going to force you to do that tonight".

"And why did you want the asteroid to hit the Earth and wipe out all life?", asked Carson.

Stacks hesitated again. Carson pressed the gun into his face. This time Hammer gave the answer.

"It was the will of God that that asteroid should strike the Earth, wipe out this wicked and adulterous generation and herald the reign of Christ".

"You're both a pair of raving madmen", said Carson. "The fact that we have destroyed the asteroid proves that it never was the will of God that it should strike the Earth. If God had really wished the Earth to be destroyed in such a way, no technology, however advanced would ever have been able to stop Him".

"Now Stacks", said Carson. "I want the answer from you, not from that half-wit over there."

"I wanted the asteroid destroyed", said Stacks. "I also wanted the debris destroyed, but I wanted to save two robots for the apocalyptic display".

"So your aim was political power then?" said Carson.

"Yes", sighed Stacks as he gazed fixedly at the floor.

"Well Stacks, you're the evil scheming politician and your buddy over there is the raving apocalyptic nut", sneered Carson.

Hammer simply grunted in contempt.

"Now Stacks", said Carson., "put the Armitage voice

synthesiser in your mouth and ask Rachel May to come in here".

Rachel walked into the office. Carson was hiding the gun behind his back. Rachel was surprised at whom she saw. Carson pointed the gun at her and motioned her over to where Stacks was sitting.

"Do you recognise anyone here Rachel?", asked Carson.

"Yes eh I mean nnnno!!" she shrieked.

Carson then pointed the gun at Stacks and said: "Then you won't mind if I shoot this man here."

"No" screamed Rachel. "Please this is my daddy", and she flung protecting arms around him.

"Thank you", said Carson. "That's all I needed to know".

"Now Rachel, be a good, sweet little girl and tell me where my wife is. Where is Sylvia?"

"She's being held in a room in the living quarters", said a frightened Rachel.

"You three lead the way", Carson ordered, "and though my gun will be concealed under these files, don't forget it's pointing at you. The first one that makes any funny move is dead. Do I make myself quite clear?"

The three muttered and mumbled "yes".

Carson yelled out: "I said 'do I make myself quite clear'?"

All answered with a more articulate and pronounced "yes".

Half way along the long corridor leading to Sylvia's place of confinement, Carson ordered the three to halt. He whispered to Stacks to inform the guard to bring Sylvia out.

A moment later the guard came out with a gun at Sylvia's head.

"Drop your gun Carson or I'll shoot your wife?" shouted the guard.

Stacks turned round and said "I think you'll see reason

now Carson". He took a couple of steps forward and said "now hand over that gun. And then let's go to the control room and change the co-ordinates on those missiles as we originally planned – unless of course you want Sylvia dead".

"One more step and I'll pull the trigger", shouted Carson.

"I'll shoot this instant", yelled the guard.

"Then shoot away", said Carson quite calmly and collectedly.

"I, I,… I mean what I say", said the guard.

"No I don't think you do", said Carson.

"I mean it, I'll shoot your wife right now", continued the guard.

"Then prove your sincerity by shooting her", said Carson. "Or", continued Carson, "I'll shoot her myself after I've shot you".

"You're bluffing", said Hammer.

"No" said Carson. "You four are bluffing. If you want to stay alive lady, take off the mask".

The mask was removed.

"I thought it was you Rita", said Carson. "This is where you slipped up Stacks. I know Armitage better than you thought I did. His wife is named Julia, she's still alive and is in A1 health. Rita is your wife. Oh some Christian husband you are Stacks to use your wife this way. And more fool you lady. Or should I say 'not a lady."

Carson disarmed the guard and motioned him along with Stacks, Hammer and Rita into the room. He ordered Rachel to lock the door. Next, he took the key from Rachel and tried the door to ensure it was truly locked.

"Now Rachel", said Carson. "Take me to Sylvia. And this time – no tricks, that is, if you really value your life", he warned her. "Lovely and beautiful as you are, I won't hesitate to use this thing, if you say or do anything funny", he further warned her as he brandished the revolver in front of her. "Now where is Sylvia, Rachel?", demanded Carson, "And this time, the truth....or else", he added as he threateningly waved the gun in front of her face. Rachel now clearly understood that he meant business.

Rachel and Carson approached the place of Sylvia's confinement which was a cell just below the living quarters.

"Halt", cried the guard. Rachel and Carson obeyed the guard's command. They were now about three quarters of the way along the corridor leading to the cell.

"Now Rachel dearie", whispered Carson, "you know exactly what to say".

"Dr. Stacks wishes Sylvia to be brought up to the main control room", Rachel informed the guard.

"Who is the man with you?", asked the guard sternly.

"This is William Foster a medical doctor, he wants to examine Sylvia first", said Rachel.

"Your ID", said the guard rather curtly.

"Here it is", said Carson as he pointed the gun at the guard. "Now open up and bring Sylvia out".

The startled guard immediately proceeded to unlock the door.

Sylvia emerged from the room and wanted to rush into the arms of her husband.

"Harold, Harold!!", she shouted.

"Not yet, Sylvia. Not yet", cautioned Carson. "Wait 'til I deal with the guard".

Carson disarmed the guard and took his keys and cell phone.

"Now get inside", he commanded the guard. He then locked them in the room.

Carson then wheeled round and shot Sylvia dead. As she dropped to the floor, a revolver fell from her hands. Carson then unlocked the cell door and ordered the guard to take off his uniform. He then hit the guard over the head with the butt of the machine gun which he had taken from him before he locked him in the room. The guard was knocked out cold. Carson then quickly donned the uniform. When the mask on the dead girl was removed, it revealed a face Carson did not know. He guessed that she was probably one of the female workers at the base.

"I should kill you here and now", he growled at Rachel. "Lead me on a third wild goose chase and you'll join your colleague here", he said as he pointed down at Sylvia's dead impersonator.

Rachel stood outside the room where Stacks, Hammer, Rita, the guard and Sylvia were confined.

She opened the door and said "it's all over – Carson is dead"

"We heard a shot ring out from underneath", said Hammer.

"The guard shot Carson dead", said Rachel.

Stacks, Hammer, Rita and the guard emerged from the room. Carson, who was standing in the corner next to the door hard up against the wall, then revealed himself. The four were frozen to the spot with shock. Carson then bolted into the room and fired a shot.

"Get back inside – you too Rachel", said Carson.

"Sylvia – come forth", commanded Carson.

"Har darling, Oh Har, Oh Har", said Sylvia with tear filled eyes.

She walked calmly towards her husband who pulled at her face and examined her mouth. This was indeed the real Sylvia.

"You see", Carson told the five criminals, Sylvia has never ever in her life called me anything other than Har." Carson of course conveniently forgot the "pig" and "two timing swine"!! He then locked the five up again.

"How did you know there was another guard inside", Sylvia asked him

"Because", replied Harold, "I figured that if this time Rachel was telling me the truth and that you really were in that room, you would have come out after I had called the other guard's bluff over Rita. I knew that there just had to be another guard in there and that I had to act quickly and kill him."

EPILOGUE.

The Ben Nevis Base was raided by the military police. Stacks, Hammer, Rita, Rachel and the two guards were taken into custody. Nathanial Armitage was released from the crypt where he had really been confined.

"The robots located only twenty pieces of debris 100 feet and over in diameter", said Sir Charles MacDouglas to Harold, Sylvia, and Nathanial as they sat in his office at the Royal Observatory in Edinburgh. "These have now been destroyed".

"Once the pieces of debris come within Earth's orbit, we should see a rather interesting display of shooting stars", said Sylvia.

"Some rocks may be large enough to penetrate the Earth's atmosphere", warned Sir Charles.

"But hopefully not large enough to cause any real damage?", Nathanial asked.

"Most unlikely", said the Astronomer Royal. "Oh somebody might get a nasty knock on the head or a rock clattering through their living room window – but that's about the most of it", he laughed.

"We'll all wear tin helmets, just in case", said Armitage.

The following year, between October and December, the inhabitants of planet Earth were treated to the most spectacular meteor displays ever seen. The brightest, the biggest and the most spectacular and longest lasting of all was seen at midnight on 24th December by some farmers over the Shepherds' Fields near Bethlehem!

—Christmas At CERN—

Chapter 1.

No Separation of Church and Laboratory.

"Dad, we've been through all of this before", said 16 year old Raymond Davidson to his father. "I've really no interest in embarking upon a career in the church. I'm interested in science and my heart is set upon specialising in Physics."

Archibald Davidson was one of those sort of people who simply could not take "no" for an answer. As well as holding the Michael Ramsay Chair of Theology at Cambridge University , the Reverend Dr . Archibald Davidson was also an ordained Church of England clergyman. His father and grandfather before him had both been in Holy Orders and he naturally expected that his son Raymond would follow the family tradition and be a man of the cloth.

"You know Raymond, you can be both a priest and a scientist at the same time", said Archibald. "Many great scientists were priests. Nicholas Copernicus was a Dominican monk, Abbe Georges Lamiatre was a Belgian priest and Gregor Mendel, like Copernicus, wore the habit. Therefore, not only can theology and science be in perfect harmony but so can a career in both church and laboratory".

Young Raymond looked very serious for a moment. He glanced at his father and his father glanced back at him. His father could tell from his son's body language and facial expression that he had something to say which was of very great moment; he discerned from the gravity of his son's bearing that it was something which had been on his mind for a long time and that he had never, until now, managed to pluck up the courage to come straight out with it. His father waited with great anticipation.

"Look Dad, I've got something to say to you, you're not going to like it. I'd prefer if Mum were here too for this one". Patricia Davidson was also a theologian of some standing and taught Bible History at Cambridge . She left off her exam marking and came through to her husband's study to join in the discussion between her husband and son.

"I take it that this is the time when Raymond is going to inform us that he doesn't believe in God and that he has been attending church for the past couple of years simply to please us".

"Yes it is", replied her husband quite calmly and collectedly.

Raymond Davidson, wide eyed and gaping, sat frozen and speechless on his chair. Parents and offspring maintained this silence for about half a minute. Archibald and Patricia allowed their son to absorb and come to terms with what he had just heard. It was Archibald who broke the silence: "don't be surprised son, your mother and I were not born yesterday".

"But... but... hhh how could you possibly have known", Raymond stammered.

"Over the past two or three years, your father and I have noticed your enthusiasm for religion wane".

"Your bible reading and your prayers have all gone by the board and your general demeanor in church is perfectly indicative of a faith which has grown cold", continued the boy's father.

"It's just that…."

"You can't seem to reconcile science and religion", said his father finishing off his son's sentence.

Raymond, taking a deep breath, simply said "precisely".

"Raymond, you are young and you have so much to learn" explained his mother. "As you grow older and wiser, you will come to realise that science and religion are not so poles apart as you think they are".

Raymond simply stared sadly down at the ground: "sorry Dad, sorry Mum. I know you so much wanted me to go into the ministry – but I can't keep up the pretence any longer. It would be sheer hypocrisy for me to seek ordination.". Taking another deep breath, the boy continued: "I know I'm a great disappointment to you".

"So many of the Davidson family have given their sons to the church", said Archibald, "but I cannot force you to do something your heart is so set against. I can only hope and pray that one day you will see the light. You will see the light one day Raymond".

"How are you getting on with your maths?" Ruth Foster asked Raymond as they walked around the quadrangle of St. John's College Cambridge. Both Raymond and Ruth were in their first year at this ancient and venerable university – Raymond in the Faculty of Science and Ruth in the Faculty of Arts. Raymond hoped to specialise in physics and Ruth dreamed of being a philosopher.

"The maths tripos are really tough", Raymond replied to his girlfriend's question, "it's hard going and needs a lot of study".

"You look a bit down in the mouth Ray", Ruth observed of

her boyfriend. "Have you been having more arguments with your parents on the subject of religion?"

"Mum is pretty much reconciled to my atheism, but Dad is rather contradictory. On the one hand he says I must come to religion in my own way and in my own time, but on the other hand, he keeps preaching to me – sort of beating me over the head with the Bible. When that doesn't work, he then tells me how science and religion need not necessarily be mutually antagonistic."

"Well, Ray, I think he's right."

"Yes, but he's lectured me on this time out of mind. Since I admitted my atheism to him a couple of years ago, he has just never let up. I see his argument but I'm not convinced by it."

"Many great scientists were believers. Michael Faraday and Albert Einstein immediately come to mind. Sir Fred Hoyle, who was Plumian Professor of Astronomy at this University around the middle of the last century had his atheism shattered when he discovered the resonance of the carbon atom. He came to the conclusion that the Universe could not have come about by mere chance."

"Ruth, you sound like my mum and dad rolled into one".

Ruth smiled and took this as a compliment. "Come on Ray", she said, "let's have a cup of tea".

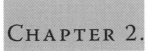

CHAPTER 2.

DECISIONS, DECISIONS

Forty years after CERN had started operating, the Higgs Boson particle remained as elusive as ever. It was supposedly the most fundamental of all the fundamental particles. Yet, in spite of the tremendous power of the CERN reactor to smash atoms to pieces, this particle had never been discovered. Many new particles had been discovered since CERN started operating in 2008 and many new insights into the sub-atomic world were made, but not even the application of the most brilliant minds in physics could produce the Higgs Boson particle.

"If you discovered this particle Ray, you'd be sure of a Nobel Prize" said Ruth Davidson to her husband as they sat in front of a blazing log fire in their villa in Geneva , Switzerland .

"That's why they made me Director of CERN Ruth. I was convinced that I could devise a way of finding this particle", said Raymond Davidson. "Perhaps it was just youthful vigour and teenage dreams. If I don't find the particle soon, I really feel I must resign as Director."

"Oh don't say that dear. You have a lot of contributions to make in the field of physics; Higgs Boson isn't everything".

"I know – but it was my whole raison d'etre for taking up

this post. Ohhh sometimes I feel that my father was right – I should have just gone into the Church,"

"I think James has made the right decision", said Ruth.

"Like grandfather, like grandson" sighed Raymond.

"If his calling is to the priesthood, you should not interfere. Remember Ray, you didn't like your own father trying to persuade you to go into Holy Orders."

"If I couldn't discover the Higgs Boson particle, I hoped James at least might."

"If your father were still alive, he'd probably say to you 'now you know what it feels like, Raymond'".

It was 10pm on December 23rd and Professor Raymond Davidson was sitting in his office in somewhat pensive mood.

"What a way to spend the Christmas season", he mused to himself.

Although Raymond did not believe in the religious aspects of the season, he enjoyed the secular feasting and rejoicing associated with the season. His office, like his home, was replete with Christmas tree, decorations and Christmas cards.

"I'm going to give it one more shot", he thought. "I'm sure I can get this collider to bombard particles at the speed of light."

Conventional wisdom always held that that would be dangerous. It could set off a nuclear explosion: it could create an expanding Black Hole: it could set off a chain reaction of…. well just about anything.

The good professor hesitated. He felt some qualms of conscience in what he saw as having to keep a balance between his own career and personal ego on the one hand and his duties to humanity on the other.

He started once again along his usual lines of reasoning.

"If the inventors of the train, car and plane had listened to the conventional wisdom of their respective days then these means of transport would never have been invented as it was generally held that the human body could never withstand such enormous speed. Unless the scientists of yesteryear had stuck their necks out a bit then we'd still be traveling around in horses and buggies." And so, Professor Davidson decided that his scientific neck was not going to remain unstuck out! He was not going to be the odd man out among the millennium's greatest scientists.

The problem had always been to achieve an acceleration at the exact speed of light. CERN scientists had managed to smash atoms into tinier and tinier pieces and had discovered a bewildering array of ever smaller fundamental particles of matter. But the Higgs Boson particle remained as elusive as ever. Raymond had always been convinced that if particles could be smashed at 186,300 miles per second, this "holy grail" of particles would reveal itself.

Raymond had devised a way of achieving bombardment at light's speed. He had held back this knowledge from his colleagues at CERN not because of a vainglorious wish to "be the first" in discovering the particle and bagging the coveted Nobel Prize which would without a modicum of doubt have come his way, but because his fellow scientists would overrule him in committee when the issue came on to the agenda. His colleagues were of the more conventional and cautious sort – at least that is how Raymond saw them. However, they considered Raymond as being of the more gung ho type. While they had great respect for their Director and highly approved of the manner he ran CERN, they often had to pull him back from his more "unconservative" ways. Raymond was determined that for "this one", he was not going to be hamstrung by bureaucracy, he was going to do this one alone.

The modifications and adaptations which Raymond had devised for the collider were the result of years of painstaking work. It was, however, only in the last six months or so that his plans were completed and ready for implementation. And so, Raymond's nocturnal hours were explained to his wife and family as being necessary for the upgrading of the collider. "Not a lie", he often comforted himself by saying. Yet, he did not even tell his own wife the true nature of the "upgrading". He did though sometimes bring Ruth and James along just to show that he was not "having an affair" with the quintessential secretary!

On this occasion, Ruth and James were with Raymond. Raymond told his wife and son that he wanted to check the new upgraded accelerator.

"Just wait here a moment", he told his family.

Raymond went into the main control room. This was the big moment – should he or shouldn't he "click that switch". Was "doing it in the name of science" merely a rationalisation ? Wasn't the truth of the matter nearer towards the satisfaction of his cravings for fame? Raymond wrestled with these conflicting emotions. He tried to sincerely convince himself that this was being done in the service of science and humanity. For a further five minutes he agonized over the panel of controls in front of him. Eventually he took a deep breath and set the collider in motion!

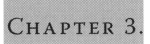

Chapter 3.

Here today, gone to yesterday.

Sweat pored off Raymond's brow. After about a minute though, he started to feel more relaxed. There was no explosion. No gaping Black Hole appeared before him. Ten minutes later, he shut down the collider and returned to his office where his family were patiently awaiting him.

"I'll let the computer analyse the results. These should be ready tomorrow morning", he thought to himself.

"Is everything all right Raymond?", Ruth asked her husband. "You're shaking – what's the matter darling?"

"I'm …I'm …all right" stammered Raymond in reply. "I was just a bit worried about eh the eh new upgraded devices …that's all".

As the three of them sat down to some coffee and biscuits, a very slight shudder was heard.

"What was that Dad?" asked James a little startled.

"Let me just check – won't be long".

"Be careful Ray", said Ruth somewhat anxiously.

"Don't worry, I'll be back in a couple of seconds", Raymond assured his family.

Raymond retraced his steps to the control room. As he entered the room, he noticed how dark it was. He could not remember turning off the lighting. He groped in the dark for the switches but could not locate them; in fact he could not locate anything – not even the walls. All sensation appeared to leave him, he could not even feel the floor underneath his feet.

About a minute later, the room started to brighten up, but it was not with the brightness of the artificial neon lights which had been installed in the room. It seemed more as if the natural brightness of the sun was illuminating the room. And yet, the objects in the room did not seem to be there. The controls, the desks, the chairs and all the paraphernalia of scientific equipment were not shown up by the light.

Raymond rubbed his eyes. Perhaps it was all the stress of the past year that was at last taking its toll on his physical and mental health. Slowly but surely, the light began to reveal objects, but they were not the objects of the control room that were revealed. Slowly but surely a picture began to emerge, but it was not the familiar picture of the control room. Raymond found himself in a completely different world. He was standing in the middle of a very dusty street. There was a market nearby with vendors zealously trying to persuade passers-by to purchase their wares. Donkeys, horses and camels plodded their way around the town. Raymond pinched himself hard to find out whether or not he was dreaming. The pain which he felt in his arm convinced him that he was perfectly compos mentis.

But what was this place? What was this alien world to which he had been so mysteriously transported? His first thought was to get back to his family. He wheeled around to find the door which would lead him out of the control room. To his shock, no door revealed itself; instead more of the same market place was presented to his eyes.

Raymond began to panic. "Excuse me, excuse me", he hysterically called out to a man leading a donkey laden with merchanidise along the dusty road. But the man simply ignored him.

"Where am I? What place is this?", he asked a stall-holder, but Raymond was greeted with the same cold-shouldering he got from the man with the donkey. Raymond continued with his attempts to glean information as to his whereabouts, but his pleas were constantly ignored. It then occurred to him – "they can't see me. That's it, *they can't see me*". In a last desperate attempt to elicit some sort of communication, Raymond decided he would have to be physical. He walked over to a cloth salesman with the intention of shaking him by the shoulders and forcing him to provide some information. Raymond extended his arms towards the cloth salesman's shoulders, but when he tried to grab him, his hands went right through him, like light through the glass on a window.

At last , Raymond calmed down. He reminded himself that he was a scientist. Yet, he was also a human being – his first thoughts were directed towards Ruth and James. His logic and rationality however told him that hysteria and panic would offer no solution to his predicament. When he had regained his senses, all his training as a scientist came out.

"Right now", he said to himself firmly, "what have I learned so far?" After a few moments of thought he came to his first conclusion: "I'm invisible to all around me. I can see my fellow human beings but they cannot see me. As to the 'whys' of this, I can figure out only with more informational input. Perhaps an easier question to answer would be 'where exactly am I?'".

Calmly and collectedly, Raymond started to explore this new and strange environment to which he had been so mysteriously transported. "From the dress of the people around me, from the wares being sold, from the architecture of the buildings and from the species of flora and fauna, I conclude that this is some sort of Middle Eastern setting".

Another question then suggested itself to Raymond: "I've noticed what there is here, but I have to consider what there is not in this mysterious place." He paused for another few moments. "Of course, there are no cars or any other form of modern transport. I see no laptops, no computers, no hi fi systems, no DVD players, no televisions or any kind of modern electronic device either being sold or used. So asking 'when am I?' has equal relevance as to 'where am I?'".

"Definitely not in the first quarter of the 21st century is an obvious conclusion. But exactly what period of Middle Eastern history have I been whisked back to?" At this point in his deliberations, school-boy memories started to invade his mind. "What is the point of studying history? What is the use of it? What can mankind gain from learning about dead people and events that have long since passed?" were the genre of question he posed to his long-suffering history teachers. Oh how he now wished he had paid more attention during these history lessons! He suddenly remembered the advice of his old headmaster Mr. Barclay. "My boy, there is no such a thing as useful or useless information. What is useful or useless in terms of information will depend upon the context in which a particular piece of information may be used. It will depend upon the situation – be it expected or unexpected - in which one may find oneself at any moment in the course of life."

What the young Raymond had hated even more than history lessons were the periods of religious instruction. As a convinced atheist, he saw no relevance in religious instruction. His attitude had always been to "grin and bear it". But he could never muster up any interest in it.

As he walked around the town, he chanced upon a

building which struck him as being somewhat familiar. He couldn't quite make out what building it was or quite where he had seen it before. Had he seen it in real life, on television or in books? He couldn't remember.

He stared and stared at the imposing edifice for at least two minutes. Then, it clicked. For the first time in his life he was grateful to his late father for all the information he had given him about this particular building. Oh how he now upbraided himself for the boredom he felt as a wet-behind-the-ears thirteen year old listening to his father "rant on" about the Temple in Jerusalem .

Chapter 4.

I Stood In Old Jerusalem.

"But which epoch of history am I in?", he asked himself. To determine this he would need more information. He started walking around the ancient city of Jerusalem . Unfortunately he did not speak any Semitic language such as Hebrew or Aramaic, so he realised he would be unable to make any discoveries through linguistic means. As he rounded a corner, he heard men shouting in a language which he vaguely recognized. It was Latin. As he approached the area where the yelling was coming from, he noticed a column of Roman soldiers marching and drilling. He wracked his brains for dates. "It cannot be earlier than 63BC when the Roman General Pompey captured Jerusalem , and it cannot be later than 70AD when Vespasian and Titus destroyed the Temple . I must be either in the closing years of the inter-testamental period or somewhere in New Testament times. But when exactly?"

For many days, Raymond explored the old city. He was able to walk through walls and doors to gain access right into the very hearths and homes of the Jerusalemites. One of the fascinating things he had discovered was that he had no craving for food, water or toilet facilities. Neither did he need any rest. It was as though his entire physiological system had been suspended at the point at which it had been when he went into the control room at CERN.

"Finding out exactly *when* I am surely holds the key to my return to CERN, the 21st century and – of course, my family", he reasoned within himself. He decided to explore the Temple and its precincts for clues.

The closer he got to this great edifice, the more awestruck he became. It was truly a majestic feature. Totally unimpeded, Raymond walked around the Women's Court, the Court of the Gentiles and the Holy Place where he saw the Hebrew priests offering their animal sacrifices to Yahweh. At last he stood outside the Holy of Holies.

"Now this will be a sight to behold", thought Raymond to himself. "I'll go in, just for the cheek of it."

As he attempted to walk through the veil separating the Sancta Sanctorum from the Holy Place some mysterious force started to hold him back. He pushed and pushed with all his might, but try as he might, he just could not get himself through that curtain.

"This is like Alice in Wonderland", he thought. "It just gets curiouser and curiouser".

He then remembered how Mrs. Clayton his Religious Education instructor had taught him that only the High Priest could enter the Holy of Holies. And, that even the High Priest was restricted to a yearly visit which was to perform certain ceremonial functions on the Day of Atonement.

" I think I'm beginning to narrow down the historical time-frame here. While I'm within the New Testament period, it must be prior to the Crucifixion for the veil of the Temple still remains intact, it has yet to be rent in twain."

Raymond's reasoning faculties were going full hammer and tongs as he stood outside the Holy of Holies.

Was all this some stage set, some practical joke that

was being played on him? No, it was far too large and sophisticated for that.

Then it struck him – "I'm sure that my exit out of here and back to my family is in some way connected to the Holy of Holies. Yes, yes!! That's it! My way back home is through the Holy of Holies. But how do I get access to it."

He tried once again to enter this most sacred of places, but again, the mysterious force kept preventing him.

"Your way home indeed is through the Holy of Holies", a voice behind Raymond said.

Raymond wheeled round in surprise and stood agape. He stood face to face with a Being of radiant splendour and angelic countenance.

"Who.. wh wh who are you?" said Raymond in stuttering voice.

The resplendent Being simply stood and stared at Raymond.

"You can see and hear me while all these other people can't", said Raymond.

"Of course I can", answered the Being. "I have been with you a very long time".

"But you've only just come to me now."

"No, I've only become visible to you now."

"Then who exactly are you. I'm not really into guessing games. How long have you been following me around?"

"For forty years".

"What?!!"

"I'm your guardian angel. I was assigned by God to watch over you. Every human who has ever been born and ever will be has a guardian angel".

"Well I'm an atheist you know", Raymond said in harsh and protesting tones.

"What you believe or disbelieve does not change reality",

answered the angel. "You are also a scientist. Isn't it plain to your reasoning and logical faculties that the predicament you are now in clearly shows a dimension beyond the physical world of sense perception?"

"How do I know you really are who you say you are?" queried a still somewhat sceptical Raymond.

"I can tell you many things that you did in your life when you thought no-one was looking?" replied the angel.

"Such as?" quizzed Raymond.

"When you stole some cakes from your mother's larder when you were ten years old?"

"But there was no-one there?"

"There was no mortal there. But I was there and I saw you. And then as recently as two weeks ago you were thinking of a sweetheart from your high school days. You were considering 'phoning her. You just managed to pull yourself back from this adulterous brink". The angel then went on to remind Raymond of his many other misdemeanors. Some he could remember, others he had forgotten.

Raymond hung his head in shame and admitted that it was all true.

"All right, all right. Enough, enough!! cried out Raymond in embarrassment. "I love Ruth very much. It's just that I was thinking of bygone years – one does that when one approaches middle age. I only wanted to talk to her, not have an extra-marital affair with her".

"God knows that and I know that".

"Now – can you please get me back to my family? Can you please do something to gain me access to the Holy of Holies?"

"There are a number of tasks which the Almighty wishes you to accomplish before you may enter His most sacred abode".

"And what exactly are these tasks? Why not simply return me to my family and the 21st century?"

"The 21st century no longer exists."

"What do you mean?"

"The experiment which you conducted at CERN went beyond even your expectations; you achieved a speed not just near to the speed of light of light but a speed which achieved the exact speed of light. This created a massive Black Hole which engulfed the entire Earth. You cannot just return to your family and the 21st century; you have to return the 21st century itself. You have to return it to the precise nanosecond before the Black Hole swallowed up Earth's space, time and matter."

Raymond stood in utter shock and horror at the revelation of the angel. When he regained control of himself he asked the angel as to why the Black Hole only appeared when he opened the control room door and not immediately after the experiment.

"Because the laws of Quantum Mechanics are related to both the position and consciousness of the observer", the angel explained. "You set up and conducted the experiment, you went to observe the results, you went to the place from where the experiment was being controlled – so you are the one who caused the Black Hole".

"But I was looking for the Higgs Boson particle, not trying to create Black Holes" Raymond protested.

"Do you remember the philosophical discussions you used to have with your son James regarding the nature of time and matter?"

"Yes of course I do", snapped Raymond.

"James has been a disappointment to you. You wanted him to be a scientist, but he has re-established the family tradition, a tradition with which you broke."

"The events of the last few...eh .. days, have convinced me of God and the supernatural. Your relating to me the events of my life which no-one but myself could possibly have seen serves to reinforce that belief. Furthermore, you showed an ability to read my thoughts regarding my reasoning about my exit from here being through the Holy of Holies. There is really no natural or rational explanation for these extraordinary phenomena. However, the life of a cleric is still not for me. My interest, nay, my passion, is for science."

"Don't you remember your father telling you that science and religion are not mutually exclusive?"

"Yes, sure I do."

"Well, the reasoning that James used during his philosophical debates with you combined with the events that are going to unfold before you will soon convince you of your late father's great wisdom."

Raymond's mind flashed back to those evenings when he and his son would engage in good-natured debate about the meaning of life. James would argue that the most fundamental particle of matter could never be found as it was always theoretically possible to subdivide matter ad infinitum. Raymond would argue that if that were so then there would have to be either one of two possibilities. Even the simplest atom, hydrogen, would have to be infinitely large and heavy, or, it could not exist at all as it would have to be constructed from an infinite number of particles. James used St. Thomas Aquinas's theory of unconditioned reality as a means to refute his father's argument. If everything depended on an infinite series of conditions then nothing could exist. If however, we accept the obvious that things do exist, then matter has to be unconditioned at some point. It has to be conditioned so as to exist and that its existence is not of infinite weight and size. This conditioning agent had to be supernatural.

It was here that Raymond totally disagreed. He felt that the discovery of the Higgs Boson (sometimes called the "God particle") would eliminate the need for the concept of unconditioned reality. The Higgs Boson would do this by explaining the difference between the massless photon, which mediates electromagnetism, and the more massive W and Z bosons which mediate the weak force. Raymond felt that this Holy Grail of particle physics would do away with the need for the supernatural!

When father and son turned their discussions to the Universe at large, James, using the same reasoning as he did for the nature of matter, pointed out that the Universe could not always have existed, it must have had a beginning and that it would have an end. If the Universe had always existed then it could not exist as everything that would exist would have to proceed from an infinite backwards regression of time. His father felt that this macrocosmic problem was tied up with the microcosmic problem. If the Higgs Boson particle could be found, then it meant that the so-called unconditioned reality was conditioned by the limits of the expansion of the Universe. Eventually the Universe would contract in upon itself and then expand again. Each expansion and contraction phase would have its own time quanta and have nothing to do with the time quanta of the previous phase thus solving the problem of infinite backwards time regression. This limit to expansion and thus infinity would condition matter to both exist and yet not to be of infinite size and weight. Likewise the nature of the Higgs Boson particle which should explain the difference between electromagnetism and the weak force would itself be the underlying cause of so-called unconditioned reality and be the fundamental cause to save the material Universe from breaking loose into infinity and thus annihilating itself in a confusion between infinite size and infinity towards non-existence.

CHAPTER 5.

IT'S WRITTEN IN THE STARS.

"Where your reasoning breaks down", said the angel, "is on what determines the nature of the Higgs Boson particle. Let us, for the sake of argument, presume that your theories concerning Higgs Boson are correct. What then is the underlying determinant of the nature of this particle? If Higgs Boson is a preventative for matter annihilating itself in infinity, then it stands to reason that infinity exists, or else the preventative safeguard of Higgs Boson would be unnecessary."

"Well you can give me answers to these questions", said a rather subdued Raymond.

"I can't", answered his guardian angel.

"But you're an angel".

"I'm not God".

"Couldn't God tell you?"

"It is neither for angels nor men to uncover all the mysteries of creation. And what man does discover he must do so by the cognitive applications of his mind, a mind which, like his soul, sets him apart from the rest of creation as the image of the Living God."

"Then why can't man know everything".

"Because he is not God and because he is a fallen creature. However, I can tell you this: when you bombarded these particles at the speed of light, you set off a chain reaction which resulted in speeds in excess of the speed of light."

"But that's impossible – it breaks all known scientific laws. If something travels faster than light then it cannot be light."

"Precisely. It is called infinity. However, not the infinity of Heaven and the supernatural order but the continuously descending infinity of a Black Hole."

"Then if this …whatever eh it is that is not light yet which travels faster than the speed of light…oh … I'm at a loss. What is the matter that achieves these fantastic speeds?"

"Oh Raymond, Raymond – it's called darkness!!"

"Well, I've often seen darkness but I've never been pulled into any time vortex or in any way perceived of speeds greater than that of light", said Raymond rather sarcastically.

"This is a darkness caused by speeds greater than that of light. Thus no light can enlighten it."

"Why are my sensations suspended? Why are my bodily functions frozen in time? Why do I walk ghost-like in this strange world to which I have been transported? I do not even make foot-prints on the dusty roads."

"Your inability to manipulate your environment is to prevent time being warped and to ensure its linear forward motion. It is therefore impossible to change the past – you can only observe it. You can compare it to a film, you can observe its contents but have no ability to effect any changes in it".

"Now about these tasks", said Raymond rather curtly.

"These will be suggested to you as you proceed along your way"

"What way?"

"That also will be suggested to you".

With that the angel disappeared.

"Wait, wait", yelled Raymond. "I know you're still there, you are my guardian angel".

It was too late, Raymond was left alone.

"Now what?" he thought. Raymond did not know which way to turn. "There are a number of questions I need to ask you. Why this particular period of time? What happens if I can't complete the tasks? What sort of knowledge do I need for these tasks?" When no response was given, Raymond simply heaved a sigh of despair.

As Raymond walked along the dusty streets of old Jerusalem , he chanced upon a group of men in heated debate. They had long white beards, priestly looking robes and they were consulting something which appeared to be a scroll. He reasoned that they were either Scribes or Pharisees, men learned in the laws of Moses. Although he could not understand their language, for some unknown reason he felt drawn towards them. Although he had not a clue what they were saying, something, he knew not what, compelled him to stand in awe and fascination of this dignified, priestly group.

All of a sudden, something happened which startled Raymond. The men started to speak in flawless English. The first man to speak appeared to be the leader of the group – perhaps the High Priest.

"We know not the resting place of the Ark of the Covenant – God will reveal it in His own good time".

"Perhaps it has been taken to Heaven in the same manner as the prophet Elijah was taken there", said another priest.

"Our ancient scriptures say nothing about this?" said the leader.

"Nevertheless, I feel that we must somehow look heavenwards if we are to discover the great mystery of the Ark. "

Raymond now understood that his task was to discover the Ark.

"Excuse me, can you hear me?, hello", he called out to the group of men. He thought that because they were speaking in his own tongue, they might be cognisant of his presence. But the men were not aware of Raymond standing close to them. "If you do not know where the Ark is how can I possibly find it", he objected.

Although the priestly group could neither see nor hear him, Raymond was astonished to hear them answer his question.

"The sign of the Ark surely must appear in the sky", said one of the priests.

"Yet we look for a living Ark ", said the leader.

"Indeed – the signs are in the stars", said another of the group.

"But there is no constellation that resembles an Ark ", Raymond cried out.

Raymond was again surprised to hear an answer to his question.

"The Greek island of exile holds the key", said the one whom Raymond termed the "High Priest".

"But the constellations are the same all over the northern hemisphere", protested Raymond.

The group remained silent.

"Well?", shouted Raymond. "Are you really so ignorant of the fundamentals of spherical astronomy?"

The group of scribes started to talk – but this time in their own dialect of Aramaic.

"Can't you speak to me in English just one more time?" Raymond hollered at them.

But the group of learned men continued to talk in their own language completely oblivious to Raymond's presence.

It occurred to Raymond that they did not actually understand English. They had spoken all the time in Aramaic, Raymond had simply "heard" them in his own native tongue. Yet they had somehow been divinely inspired to answer some of his questions!

The notion of a constellation resembling an Ark was something which Raymond dismissed from his thinking. Instead, he concentrated on "yet we look for a living Ark".

Chapter 6.

Read your Bible lad!

Just what this "living Ark " might be, Raymond simply could not imagine. Again he deeply regretted not having paid more attention during his religious studies lessons when he had been a school-boy. Try as he might, he could think of nothing in scripture, either in the Old or New Testament which in any way could be construed as a "living Ark ". He remembered what his guardian angel had told him about mankind having to use its God-given faculties to fathom out the mysteries of creation.

"Well, my good angel, I just give up. I can't fathom out this "living Ark "

All of a sudden, everything went dark. Raymond found himself caught in a kind of swirling mist. He hoped that the divine powers-that-be had given up on him as a "theology student" and, having him down as a "doctrinal dunce" were going to dump him like a sack of potatoes back at CERN. This however turned out to be mere wishful thinking. When the mist cleared, Raymond found himself in the same biblical Middle Eastern setting but in a different city. It appeared to be rather small – more a village than a city he thought. As he proceeded forward his foot hit something which almost caused him to fall. This immediately occurred to him as strange as nothing was supposed to be tangible to him. When he looked down on the dusty rock-strewn road, Raymond saw a book. He picked up the book and saw the words "Holy Bible – Douay Rheims Version" written on the front outside cover.

This seemed odd to Raymond. He had sufficient knowledge of the period to understand that during this period of human development, writing was contained in the form of scrolls, not bound books with pages. However, he realised that the out-of-period book form and its tangibility was a help from Heaven to guide him on his way and to assist him in the completion of his tasks.

"But what is this Douay Rheims version?", he asked himself. He had never heard of this version of the Bible before. As he perused its first few pages, he learned that it was the first Roman Catholic vernacular version of the Bible published at the College of Rheims in France in 1582.

"I wonder why this particular version", he mused. "it must have something to do with Catholic theology. Now what separates Catholics from non-Catholics".

Raymond felt that successfully answering this question would lead help him progress in his tasks. He pondered the questions of transubstantiation, papal infallibility, the doctrine of original sin, the sacrificial nature of the Mass, apostolic succession, church hierarchy and many others. Nothing, though pointed him on his route to further progress in his quest.

"Of course!", he suddenly yelled out. "How stupid of me – I forgot the Virgin Mary. Catholics pay great honour and veneration to the Virgin as the Mother of God."

This time Raymond realised he had hit the nail on the head. Along the dusty street, a humble little house glowed with an un-Earthly glow. Raymond walked towards it. As he entered in, he saw a young girl of about 16 or 17 years of age kneeling before a magnificent angel. They spoke to each other in a language Raymond could not understand. However, before the angel departed Raymond heard the final words in English, words which he knew so well: "Behold the hand maid of the Lord. Be it done unto me according to thy word".

"That must be it", thought Raymond, "the Virgin Mary is the 'living Ark ' This town must be Nazareth ".

If Raymond thought that that would be good enough to have him moved on to his next task, he was sadly deluded. All that happened was the sound of a disembodied voice which simply uttered one word "how?"

"Ah yes, of course", thought Raymond. "That's why I've been given a Bible".

Raymond spent many days studying all the texts which referred to the Ark of the Covenant of the ancient Israelites. The great question before him was – how do these texts refer to the Blessed Virgin Mary? He vaguely remembered an exegetical technique known as "typology". This meant finding texts in the Old Testament whose persons, places and objects point towards the same in the New Testament.

As he was reading through Exodus 40, verse 32 caused him to pause and reflect. "The cloud covered the tabernacle of the testimony and the glory of the Lord filled it".

"That's it, that's it", said Raymond excitedly and he hurried forward to St. Luke Chapter 1 verse 35 "And the angel answering said unto her: The Holy Ghost shall come upon thee, and the power of the most High shall overshadow thee. And therefore also the Holy which shall be born of thee shall be called the Son of God."

"There is the parallel" , reasoned Raymond. "The Ark of the Covenant typifies the Virgin Mary".

It all then started to fall into place for Raymond. The

Ark contained the 10 Commandments written in stone; the womb of the Virgin contained Jesus Who is the living word of the living God come in the flesh. The Ark contained a pot of manna; Jesus was the living bread come down from Heaven. The Ark contained Aaron's rod that came to life; Jesus was "the Branch" who would die and return to life after three days. "The Branch" was a Messianic title. Jesus was a branch of the Davidic line as was His mother Mary and His foster-father, St. Joseph . As the blossoming branch signified Aaron as the true and rightful High Priest, so would Jesus' resurrection after three days confirm Him as the true and eternal High Priest.

Raymond must have made satisfactory progress in his studies as, once again the swirling mist surrounded him and the little town of Nazareth disappeared from before his eyes. He clearly understood that he was being moved on to his next task and not back to CERN and his family.

When the mist cleared, Raymond found himself in hilly countryside. As he looked around, he espied many tiny hamlets and lonely little houses. Here and there shepherds tended their flocks and women and children the small vegetable patches and fruit trees around their quaint little homes.

Raymond realised that he would need to study his Bible more before he could find out in which direction he ought to travel.

"Now, what has hilly topography got to do with the Ark of the Covenant", muttered Raymond to himself.

After much searching, Raymond came to the Second Book of Samuel in which verses 1 – 11 of Chapter 6 describe how the Ark traveled to the hill country of Judah to rest in the house of Obed-edom.

"So how I wonder does this connect to Mary in the New Testament."

Raymond thought long and hard on this one but could not figure it out. He proceeded to ask himself this question: "Where did Mary go after the annunciation?" After a only a few seconds, it dawned on him – "Of course, to her cousin Elizabeth in the hill country of Judah ."

A small hamlet on the top of a nearby hill lit up with that same heavenly glow which had lit up the little house in Nazareth . Raymond made towards it as fast as his legs could carry him.

Once there, he saw Mary and Elizabeth greet each other. The only word he understood was "shalom". However, the words in this exchange between Mary and Elizabeth which were revealed to Raymond in English were what he recognised as his cue to further scriptural analysis.

"Blessed art thou among women, and blessed is the fruit of thy womb. And whence is this to me, that the mother of my Lord should come to me? For behold as soon as the voice of thy salutation sounded in my ears, the infant in my womb leaped for joy".

This time Raymond had to go back to the Old Testament to find the parallels. As Elizabeth wondered at how she could be privileged with a visit from the Mother of her Lord, so King David in 2 Samuel 6 :9 was recorded as having said: "How shall the ark of the Lord come to me?" St. John the Baptist who was a priest's son, and who would become a priest in later years, leapt for joy in his mother Elizabeth's womb when Mary came into the presence of Elizabeth, so did King David clad in priestly attire ecstatically dance before the Ark of the Lord.(2 Samuel 6:14) Just as Elizabeth shouted for joy at the visit of Mary so did David cry out for joy in the presence of the Ark.(2 Samuel 6:15)

The Ark of the Covenant remained three months in the house of Obed-edom. Mary remained with Elizabeth for three months.

Raymond found in 2 Samuel 6 12 and 3 Kings 8: 9 – 11 that when the Ark returned to its sanctuary and eventually to the Temple in Jerusalem , the presence and the glory of God were revealed. Eventually Mary would return to her own home from the house of Elizabeth and after her sojourn in Bethlehem , present the Son of God in the Temple in Jerusalem .

Raymond found that in verses 4 – 6 of the fourth chapter of the Book of Numbers, the Ark was always covered with a blue veil when it was taken outside of the Holy of Holies.

"Of course", Raymond exclaimed, "blue is the colour of the Virgin Mary. Those who have seen her outside of Heaven, usually describe her as wearing a blue veil".

Raymond took the mist that now started to envelop him as an indication that he had completed this second task with flying colours. He wondered what would be the next stop.

CHAPTER 7.

THE STARS AT NIGHT
ARE BIG AND BRIGHT

After the mist had cleared, Raymond found himself standing in a bleak and windswept place. It was just as well that his body was immune from the elements as this place seemed bitterly cold and barren. The sea was nearby and he watched its mighty waves come crashing onto the seashore.

"Where and what is this wilderness?", Raymond asked himself. He then remembered the words of the chief of that group of elders whom he had encountered when he was in Jerusalem : "the Greek island of exile holds the key".

"This must be the place. But where exactly am I? What has all this to do with the Virgin Mary and a constellation resembling the Ark".

Nothing made any sense to him. He decided to explore his surroundings for any signs of clues which could help.

The island appeared to be uninhabited; apart from the birds flying overhead and letting loose their mournful caws and a few lizards scurrying to and fro, he was, at least as far as he could see, the only human being on the island. After about a half an hour's walking, he espied a cave a few hundred yards away. As he approached its mouth, he was pleasantly surprised to see a human like figure emerge from it. As he drew nearer, he descried an extremely old man. With his long white beard and wisps of white hair, he looked at least 90 years old.

"What on Earth is a man of his age doing in such a place as this?"

That the old man could not see him had less to do with his diminished vision due to age and more to do with Raymond being invisible to those who were in his presence. When Raymond entered the cave, he saw a quill pen, ink and ancient writing parchments.

Raymond decided that he would stay put. Surely this man somehow held the answer to his searches. He started to observe the actions of this elderly and venerable man. The man's actions struck Raymond as being strange. He looked up at the sky for at least two minutes and then went into the cave and wrote a few sentences on the parchment. From the torchlight, Raymond could see that the script was Greek. He recognised the characters but could not discern the meaning.

The old man repeated this action at least ten times. Each astronomical observation was longer than the preceding one and each session over the parchment likewise longer than the one before. Raymond joined the old man in his star gazing. There did not seem to him anything unusual in the constellation patterns. Yet, something was grabbing the old man's fascination.

It suddenly clicked.

"How slow of me, how dull-witted I am. This man must be St. John banished to the island of Patmos ."

Now it became clear exactly what the "island of exile" meant. But what was the seer looking at in the sky?

Raymond went to the last book in the Bible and looked up the final verse of Chapter 11. It describes St. John as seeing the Ark of the Covenant in Heaven. Chapter 12 tells of the woman standing with the moon beneath her feet and she is crowned with twelve stars and clothed with the sun. But as Raymond looked up into the sky he saw nothing that looked like an Ark and nothing like a woman standing on the moon. He looked again more closely and saw that the constellation rising in the east behind Leo was Virgo. There was a new moon which was indeed at the "feet" of Virgo.

"This must surely symbolise the Virgin Mary. The new moon heralds in the Jewish new year. Because Virgo rises behind Leo, she is symbolically 'clothed with the sun'". It all started to fall into place. A new year and a new moon signifying a new birth. It was of course the Virgin Birth. Yet, there was something still missing. John's exile on Patmos occurred about 100 years after the birth of Christ. Oh how Raymond wished he had the appropriate computer software which could show him the sky at any period in the Earth's history! He realised that he was going to have to do all this the hard way. He had his pen with him, some pieces of blank paper and the blank pages for notes on the back of the Bible. He commenced upon a long and laborious pen and ink job on calculating the movements of the stars right back to the time of the birth of Christ.

It was three days before Raymond had fully worked out the sky map for the closing years of the first century BC. He discovered that what St. John in the Book of the Apocalypse had seen was the same as what had occurred in the years 3BC and 2BC. In September of 2BC, the planet Jupiter came into a close conjunction with the star Regulus. Jupiter "crowned" Regulus as the apparent position of the two celestial bodies indicated that Jupiter was above Regulus.

"That's it", said Raymond to himself. "I believe I've hit on it. Jupiter, the king of the planets meets Regulus, the king of the stars. This definitely indicates kingship in some way." Raymond's painstaking calculations showed that the wobbles of Jupiter's apparent motion relative to Regulus meant that the conjunction in the year 3BC was particularly close. He also discovered that in that year the retrograde motion of Jupiter relative to the fixed background of stars resulted in the planet moving back towards Regulas for a second "coronation". Jupiter then continued on its way, but retrograde motion kicked in one more time and Jupiter once more moved backwards to meet Regulus thus to effect a third "coronation".

What Raymond found particularly interesting was that this triple crowning occurred within the constellation of Leo. The ancient Jewish prophecies foretold that the Messiah would come out of the tribe of Judah – and Judah's symbol was the lion. Raymond combined the 3BC/2BC stellar imagery with St. John's . Virgo, with the new moon at her feet symbolised a birth. And it was a virgin birth. He immediately turned the pages of his Bible to the great prophecy of Isaiah, "behold a virgin shall conceive and bear a son".

Raymond felt he deserved a pat on the back for this. He thought that that mist would start to envelop him and whisk him off to his next task. In this he was to be sadly disappointed. Disappointment soon gave way to frustration, and this in turn gave way to anger.

"Well, isn't that good enough", he screamed at his invisible guardian angel. His outburst produced no angelic response and Raymond's mood now moved from one of anger to despondency. After about half an hour of sulking with the celestial, Raymond realised that he would have to get back to his work on the star charts.

In June of 2BC, another great sign appeared in the heavens; Jupiter made a rendezvous with the planet Venus. This would have resulted in a conjunction of amazing brightness. To the ancients, Venus was the mother of the planets. Raymond superimposed this maternity on the Virgin Mary who was to be the mother of the Messiah.

Raymond felt he had been abandoned by the immortal powers that were watching over him. It was clear that there was something he was not quite hitting on. But what? An hour of contemplation and thought helped Raymond come up with this question: could this all have anything to do with the Star of Bethlehem? It could or it could not, but Raymond decided to work upon the assumption that there was here a connection. Again, he thought long and hard on this. It suddenly dawned on him. The stellar pageantry indicated the birth of a king, but the association of Leo the lion indicated specifically a Jewish king. If the planetary movements against the constellations had any sort of connection with the Star of Bethlehem which indicated the birth of a new king, then the three kings – the Magi – who trekked over "field and fountain, moor and mountain" must also be indicated in this stellar play.

Raymond thought upon the Magi for some time. He remembered that tradition held them to be kings, and the Bible termed them Magi, or wise men. But they must have been particularly wise in the science of astronomy. Three men who were at once kings, wise and astronomers. Three men with three attributes. Three, three, three! That number kept flashing at Raymond in his mind's eye. At last, the penny dropped; the triple coronation of Regulus by Jupiter, though a strong indication of the importance of the king it foretold, secondarily pointed to three kings who would travel from far and distant lands to pay their homage to the One Who is the King of kings and Lord of lords.

The longed for mist at last came and Raymond was on his way to his next task.

Chapter 8.

Bring on the Kings.

The scene now had completely changed. The barren rockiness of Patmos had given way to a hot, dry desert. It was lucky for Raymond that his physiological functions were all suspended or he would soon have died of heat stroke and dehydration. He looked all around himself and anticipated what was coming up next. He thought that at just any moment now the three kings with their pack camels and royal trains would come into view over one of the sand dunes. He waited for at least an hour, but this Christmas card scene did not materialise. Yet he well knew that his association of the triple coronation with the three kings meant that his new task involved following them on their journey to Bethlehem.

Raymond thought about the kings and how they made the long journey to worship the babe of Bethlehem . He soon realised that he would have to turn his thoughts away from glittery Christmas card scenes and the great masterpieces by Leonardo and Botticelli who treated on this theme with paint and canvass. Once again, Raymond resorted to his Bible.

Although Raymond had never been interested in such things as Biblical analyses and exegesis, his scientific training had, nevertheless provided him with a sharp and penetrating mind. Applying his critical faculties to the passages in St.

Matthew's gospel, Raymond made a number of interesting observations about the story of the wise men. First of all, the gospel account was silent as to the country or countries from which they came. Although the three kings were probably received in a common audience at Herod's court, there was nothing in scripture to support the generally accepted idea that they had journeyed together to Palestine . In fact, Raymond realised that St. Matthew had nothing to say about the actual number of wise men who visited Jesus. Tradition had always held that there were three. This assumption came from the gifts of gold, myrrh, and frankincense – one gift from each of the kings. Yet, it could only be deduced from the gospel account that there were more than just one wise man, or king. There may have been two or two hundred and two!!

"I think that this task requires me to find my way to Bethlehem, just as the kings did", Raymond thought out loud half hoping that someone would somehow hear him and at least give him some clues as to what to do next.

"I have to start walking", he said. The problem was – to where?

Night fell and the stars revealed themselves in all their glory. Raymond had often wondered why none of the modern day Gulf states had cottoned on to the idea of building an astronomical observatory. Of the 365 days in the year, only around 86 are any good for observation. This is mainly because of adverse weather conditions. But when clear skies coincide with a full moon, observing conditions are still hampered. Although there would of course still be full moons in the Middle East , there would be very few days which were clouded over. Raymond had reasoned that an astronomical observatory in any Gulf state would be a big boost to the technological development of that state and of course ultimately to its economy especially in the post-oil era. Astronomers from all over the world would flock to that state in order to take advantage of the near pristine observing conditions. As well as the science of astronomy itself, there would be spin-offs into other sciences such as physics, chemistry, astrobiology, optics and engineering.

However, Raymond snapped himself out of this reverie and attempted to apply himself to the task at hand. He surveyed his surroundings and concluded that he must be either in the Arabian Peninsula or in Persia .

"Somehow I have to get myself to Bethlehem."

He then realised that he could use the constellations to guide him on his way. In this he was greatly assisted by witnessing the astronomical phenomena he had so painstakingly worked out on the island of Patmos . For many weeks and months Raymond walked towards the Holy Land guided by the starry wonders being played out above him.

Day after day, week after week, and month after month, Raymond hoped to encounter the Magi. He saw sights which historians would give their right arms to see. The ancient Persian and Babylonian cites had him awe-struck. Their temples and palaces were magnificent. At times, Raymond had to remind himself that he was not a tourist, he was essentially a pilgrim with a place to reach and a mission to accomplish. But he was only human and he could not help but be absolutely amazed by the sights that presented themselves before his eyes.

However, Raymond very often experienced pangs of guilt. Here he was beginning to enjoy his little stint in the Biblical Middle East when his family and indeed his whole world had been swallowed up in a Black Hole, a Hole which his experiment had caused. It was these bouts of remorse which drove him on towards the Holy land .

As Raymond was able to glide ghost like on his journey,

unimpeded by the topographical features which would have hindered "flesh and blood" travelers, he reached Bethlehem in only three weeks. His job now was to search for the Holy Family. He opened his Bible at St. Matthew's gospel. He noted that the three kings entered a "house" not a "stable". So Raymond started scouting around the houses of Bethlehem but saw no-one that he thought could have passed for Jesus, Mary and Joseph.

Raymond thought that he was being somewhat "clever" by dismissing the well-known Christmas scene; the stable, the straw, the ox and ass and the other animals were no-where to be found in the gospel accounts of the birth of Jesus. His manner of reasoning about the wise men was transferred to the nativity scene. But he saw no-one resembling kings or sages entering houses. He then saw an aged shepherd leading a number of sheep along the dusty road. It then occurred to him that the best way to find the new born Infant would be to follow the shepherds from the Shepherds' Field on the outskirts of Bethlehem . The stable started to look more like a possibility after all.

After days of searching, Raymond found four shepherds attending a fairly large flock of sheep. He was convinced that he had successfully located the Shepherd's Field and the particular shepherds who were told by the angel about the birth of the Messiah. Night after night for weeks on end, Raymond hung out with the shepherds. No angel appeared. No heavenly choir was heard singing in the night sky. He counseled himself that he would have to exercise patience. Unfortunately patience was not one of Raymond's great virtues. After keeping nightly vigil for two months, Raymond decided to look again at his astronomical calculations. He discovered that on December 25th 2BC Jupiter entered retrograde motion once more and came to a halt. So, he realised that he must have arrived in

David's city before this date. From the configuration of the constellations in the night sky, he calculated that it was now December, but December 3BC.

At last, Raymond decided that there was no point in hanging around for another year. He had concluded that Jupiter was the "Star of Bethlehem" but that it would not point to where the Child lay until December 25th of 3BC. Viewed from Jerusalem the star would appear to be over the city of Bethlehem . However, this would not be for another year. Raymond started to walk away from the shepherds leaving them on their lonely vigil. He wondered how he would spend an entire year until he could once again join the shepherds and follow them to the place of Jesus' birth. He decided that he would do the "tourist bit" more intensively. What a wealth of information he would be able to gather. He would be as famous a Biblical scholar as he was a scientist. He would study the Bible and he would even try to learn a little of the language. But there was another thought that struck Raymond. Surely he should pray, pray for guidance and deliverance. Raymond had never prayed since he was about 12 years old.

"It's never too late", he thought. Humility, like patience, had likewise never been a virtue of Raymond's. His mind went back to his early childhood when he did pray regularly. Drawing on his store of childhood memories, Raymond decided that he ought to re-train himself in the art of prayer. His experiences of the past three months had now convinced him that there was a God, and that this God was omnipotent and omniscient. He controlled all of creation.

"Since this appalling disaster with the CERN collider, I've only addressed my guardian angel in harsh and sarcastic tones. I've only thought about getting out of this predicament. My selfishness has been compounded where humility should have switched on. Over the past three months, I have been obsessed with Biblical exegesis, not for the sake of advancing in the Christian faith, but for finding the clues to get me out of here and back to my own selfish little world and my own selfish little atheistic way of life."

As Raymond dried his now tear-filled eyes, he realised that he was in a very confined space. It must have measured only three feet by three feet. In front of him was a grill covered by a curtain. Next to the curtained grill was a prie dieu. He was clearly inside a confessional box. At once he knelt down and slowly but surely raised his right hand to his brow and said "In the name of the Father, and of the Son and of the Holy Ghost Amen. Bless me father for I have sinned. It has been nearly thirty years since my last confession."

Raymond then spent the next half hour recounting as best as he could all his sins since early adolescence. His family had been of the Anglo-Catholic or High Church tradition in the Church of England so he was well aware of how to make an auricular confession.

At last he saw the silhouette of the priest through the veil raise his right hand and pronounce the words of absolution.

When he stepped out of the confessional box and into the Shepherd's Field, Raymond would have appeared to anyone who had seen him to have been profoundly shaken. When he heard the words of absolution pronounced, he understood that when he had previously said "bless me father" at the commencement of his confession, the word "father" meant more than just the spiritual fatherhood of the priest. The confessional box disappeared and there was his natural father standing before him.

At last, Raymond's strength gave way. He fell to his knees before his father.

"Dad, Dad, help me, help me", he sobbed

On top of the Bible that Raymond was carrying a rosary suddenly appeared

"Say it every day Raymond. Continue with the tasks assigned to you, but do so with prayerfulness and humility. Recite the complete psalter of the Virgin Mary every day of your life." With that, the spectre of his father disappeared and Raymond recalled the prophetic words his father had spoken to him all those years ago – "You will see the light".

From that moment on, Raymond resolved upon an amendment of life and to recite Our Lady's psalter every day. He decided that he would spend the following year in prayer and study as he awaited the birth of His Saviour and the arrival of the kings. As he was about to make his way towards Bethlehem , something most unexpected happened which startled him. Not only did it startle Raymond but the shepherd's also. The field lit up and a thunderous voice spoke to the shepherds. It was the angel of God announcing the birth of the Messiah. Then the entire sky was ablaze with the whole heavenly choir. Raymond had never heard such glorious music. Not all the sopranos and orchestras in the world could match it. Raymond followed the shepherds, when, as their fear gave way to great joy, they hurried to see the new-born King of the Jews.

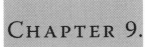

Chapter 9.

Venite Adoremus.

The shepherds led Raymond to a large tower. This appeared rather odd. It resembled neither a stable nor a house. However, as the shepherds approached the tower, Raymond noticed that they entered a small cave like structure at the tower's base.

"Ah, this must be the stable where Jesus is born. But I wonder what this tower is".

Some unseen force stopped Raymond in his tracks. His Bible mysteriously opened at the Old Testament prophecy of Micheas 4 verse 8: "And thou, O cloudy tower of the flock, of the daughter of Sion, unto thee shall it come: yea the first power shall come, the kingdom to the daughter of Jerusalem."

More and more of Raymond's religious education came back to him.

"This must be the tower of Migdal Edar . It must be what has often been termed 'the Tower of the Flock'".

It all began to make sense. This tower stood on what was then the outskirts of present day Bethlehem . It was connected with the sacrificial system of the Jerusalem Temple . The sheep in this field were specially designated for the Temple and the shepherds in this particular field had a special commission to care for the Temple 's sacrificial sheep.

The shepherds thus maintained a special ceremonially clean place for the birthing of ewes.

The theological connection now became clear to Raymond. Jesus, the perfect sacrificial lamb, the Lamb of God, would indeed have been born in the stable underneath the tower. Here is where the present day Church of the Nativity stood.

As Raymond cast his eyes upon the entrance to the cave, he noticed that it glowed. However, this glow was quite different from any Earthly light he had ever seen. As a scientist, Raymond had studied the properties of light, he knew the electromagnetic spectrum very well and had often lectured on the nature of light. His interest in astronomy had taken him to some of the biggest optical telescopes in the world. He had marveled at the many different colours which the cosmos presented and he marveled at the dazzling light given out by the vast array of stars and galaxies. But this light surpassed them all. Nothing which he had seen in the cosmos came even close to this light. It held Raymond spellbound.

The unseen force gave way and allowed Raymond to proceed. He approached the cave still in utter amazement of its unearthly glow. Before entering the sacred grotto, Raymond decided to prepare himself by prayer. He recited the entire psalter of the Virgin Mary (the three mysteries of the Rosary) and asked God the Father to make him humble in front of His Son.

Slowly and with great reverence Raymond entered the cave and stood in awe-struck wonder as he gazed upon the face of the Son of God. Time seemed to stand still for Raymond. He could only stare at the Child in the manger. He had never seen such a beautiful and radiant face. He felt that he could have stood forever in front of the crib. When he looked at Mary and St. Joseph , Raymond felt a maternal and paternal warmth emanate from them. They were not just his mother and father but the parents of his parents and of his own wife and child. For another half hour, which to Raymond seemed only like seconds, he just stood in reverend contemplation of the Holy Family of Jesus, Mary and Joseph.

Our Lady and St. Joseph took it in turn to cradle the Baby in their arms. The Child periodically woke and slept but did not cry. Joseph gathered straw to keep the Infant warm while Mary tenderly stroked the head of her Child.

The shepherds also gazed in wonder at "this thing which has come to pass". At the end of this holy hour of contemplation of God's Son, the shepherds entered into deep conversation with Mary and Joseph, but it was in a language which Raymond could not understand.

After fifteen more minutes, the shepherds left and returned to their flocks. The Virgin Mary then approached Raymond. She looked straight into his eyes. It was as if She could see him. Yet, Raymond did not think that She could possibly see him. After all, he was only a spectator of the events which had happened two thousand years ago. To his great astonishment, the Virgin Mary spoke to him.

"Never doubt that I am your mother and that I am always with you", the Virgin told Raymond.

"And never doubt that I will always be a spiritual father to you, Raymond", the foster-father of God added.

Raymond was too awe-struck to say anything.

"Go to Jerusalem and prayerfully await", said the Blessed Mother. And with that, Raymond was carried by angels to Jerusalem .

"I wonder what I have to await for", he thought. "It must surely be for the wise men".

Raymond thought again about the star. When he had seen the stellar drama in Persia , it had signaled a royal Jewish birth. However, if Jupiter were not to be seen over Bethlehem for another year, how would the Magi find the child this year.

Once again, Raymond realised that he would have to snap out of what he now termed "Christmas card thinking".

After much prayer, contemplation and study, Raymond came to understand that in the Bible, time-spans of months or even of years could be "crunched" into a few verses. It was not so much that he had missed the kings but that they, in a manner of speaking had missed him. While Raymond could almost "float" his way around the region, the kings would need to travel slowly with long trains of camels and courtly retainers. It would take them at least a year to reach Palestine .

For the next year, Raymond spent his time in prayer, contemplation and Bible study. He explored Jerusalem and learned much about the people and their customs. One day, he saw the shepherds whom he had followed to the stable in the Tower of the Flock at Migdal Edar take a consignment of sacrificial lambs to the Temple to be slaughtered. He loved to visit the Temple and watch the various rituals and ceremonials associated with its worship. With much longing, he looked towards the Holy of Holies and remembered the words of his guardian angel almost a year before "your way home indeed is through the Holy of Holies". But Raymond knew that his tasks were not yet complete and that he must not even attempt to enter this most sacred part of the Temple .

By September, Raymond decided to take up residence in the palace of King Herod . This was not because of his desire for luxury and opulence; as he had no sense of feeling and because his bodily functions had shut down, he would not have been able to take advantage of the luxury and comfort they could offer to flesh and blood. Raymond wished to be present when the Magi appeared in audience before Herod so that he could follow them to Bethlehem .

There were indeed only three who turned up at Herod's court. They were not only wise men but kings also. Although he did not understand the conversation between Herod and the kings, Raymond could see the evil and shiftiness in this ruler's eyes. After the audience, Raymond walked with the kings along the road to Bethlehem . He looked up into the night sky and saw that Jupiter's retrograde motion had stopped and that its apparent position from Jerusalem was over the town of Bethlehem .

As the royal train went through the Shepherd's Fields it took a turning away from the Tower of the Flock. Raymond was puzzled by this. If only the kings were aware of his presence he would have shouted something like "you're going in the wrong direction", but he had no choice but to follow the royal train in ghostly silence.

The kings with their camels and retainers went straight into the town of Bethlehem and made their way towards a rather humble looking house. It suddenly dawned on Raymond. "This is the 'house' of which St. Matthew wrote." Of course, the Holy Family had moved from the stable under the Tower of the Flock and into a house. The chronological crunching in Matthew's gospel meant that the Magi visited the Infant Jesus a year after His birth. Raymond had not totally got rid of his "Christmas card thinking".

"It should have been so obvious to me", he scolded himself. "Manger sets and Christmas cards depict shepherds and wise men as being all together in the stable and at the same time".

The three kings presented their precious gifts of gold, myrrh and frankincense before the Infant King. The gold represented Christ's Kingship, the gift of frankincense acknowledged his Deity - prayers like incense float heavenwards to God – and the myrrh symbolised the bitterness of His Passion and Death. For a reason unknown to Raymond, he concentrated upon the myrrh. At once the familiar mist came upon him and he was spirited away to perform his next task.

Chapter 10.

And the darkness
comprehended it not.

The scene before Raymond was now dark and foreboding. It was however, not the sort of darkness that one would normally associate with night. It was as though one could actually "cut" the darkness with a knife. There was no sun, no moon, not even any stars. Raymond had no idea at all as to where he was. It was not only the darkness which was so strange but the eerie silence which accompanied it.

"This is a sort of darkness that I have never seen. This is a silence which I have never experienced before".

It was then that Raymond heard a noise behind him. It was like the sound of something tearing – something made of cloth. Yet, Raymond could see nothing.

It then dawned on Raymond: "This must be the scene of the Crucifixion. This must surely be the three hours darkness which occurred after the death of the Saviour. I shall have to wait here until the three hours have passed."

Raymond decided to spend the three hours in prayer and contemplation. He thought about the Passion and Death of Christ. With great sorrow he realised that his own sins had contributed so much to the horrific wounds inflicted upon the body of the Lord. Here was a Death from which very nature itself had fled in absolute terror. No wonder – this was nothing less than the crime of deicide.

When the three hours darkness was over, Raymond found that he was standing on a hill. In the distance he could see another hill upon which were three crosses. His eyes became affixed upon the Cross in the centre. He stood and watched as the Body of the Lord was removed from the Cross and taken to a nearby sepulchre. Raymond felt that it was just as well that he saw this scene at a distance and in silhouette. He knew that he just couldn't bear to witness the true horrors of the Crucifixion. And there was something else that Raymond couldn't bear – the thought that his sins, especially the denial of his Saviour, had been the cause of such suffering and pain. He thought about St. Peter's denial of his Lord and realised that there are so many " St. Peters " in the world – not least of all Raymond himself.

After the burial of the Lord, the "tear" noise came into Raymond's mind. He understood that it surely had some meaning for it was the only sound he had heard during that long three hours of waiting.

Looking around himself, the scene became familiar again. He found that he was standing on Temple Mount . As he turned around he discovered that he was standing outside the Holy of Holies. This time however, there was a marked and most profound difference. The curtain separating the Holy of Holies from the rest of the Temple complex was torn in two.

"Yes, yes of course", said Raymond excitedly. "That noise I heard was the veil of the Temple which was rent in two when Christ died".

It was then that Raymond wondered if he could now go home. Surely this indicated that his mission was accomplished and that he now could exit through the Holy of Holies as his guardian angel had told him.

After saying a few prayers of thanksgiving, Raymond reverently stepped into the Holy of Holies. He saw the Table of the Loaves of Proposition and the magnificent seven branched candlestick called the Menorah. The Ark of the Covenant was no longer there of course as it had been hidden by the Prophet Jeremiah during the time of the Babylonian onslaught. Raymond gazed upon these great and glorious furnishings and felt so privileged to be in such a place.

When Raymond had taken in the glories of the Holy of Holies, he expected to be whisked home by that mysterious mist which had transported him to so many times and places. In this hope, Raymond was to be sorely disappointed for nothing happened. He stood for half an hour in the Holy of Holies praying that God would return him to his family and to the familiar surroundings of the 21st century.

"It seems that there is something else that I'm not quite getting", Raymond thought.

He stepped out of the Holy of Holies and encountered a number of priests and Temple officers ranting and raving about the mishap to the curtain. Raymond walked past them paying no attention to their indignant shrieks and screams.

He walked down the Temple Mount and sat on the ground outside the Temple 's main gate and went into deep and profound thought. When he had seen the torn curtain, his reasoning had been that Christ's Death would have made the Holy of Holies accessible to all. Christ's atonement on the Cross meant that entry into the Most Holy Place ceased to be the singular privilege of the High Priest. In this he was right, for he stood, unknown to anyone except Heaven, inside what had been the holiest place on Earth.

"That's it, that's just it" said Raymond to himself. "Of course, it 'had been' the most holy place."

What Raymond now realised was that it no longer was the Holy of Holies! Yet the angel had told him that his way home was through the Holy of Holies.

After more thought and contemplation, Raymond came to the conclusion that the Holy of Holies of which his guardian angel spoke was not the Holy of Holies associated with the Jerusalem Temple .

"What then is the Holy of Holies? Where is the Holy of Holies?" Then Raymond asked a more pertinent question – "WHO is the Holy of Holies?" Raymond decided that he would make haste to Christ's tomb.

However, as he tried to move, a mysterious force prevented him. He then heard a voice say "why seek thee the living with the dead?". Raymond recognised the voice of his guardian angel. Christ indeed is the Holy of Holies, but His tomb was not to be considered as an answer to his question "where?"

A few seconds later, more vignettes of wise counsel invaded Raymond's ears: "you can be both a priest and a scientist", "theology and science can be in perfect harmony", "you can't seem to reconcile science and religion, but now you must be aware that science and religion are not so poles apart", "I can only hope and pray that one day you will see the light. You will see the light one day Raymond". It was the voice of his father, a blast from the past!

Raymond reflected upon the words he had just heard. But what suddenly made him sit up were the words of his father. They kept coming at him and coming at him with ever greater force - "I can only hope and pray that one day you will see the light. You will see the light one day Raymond".

"The light, the light, the light, the light.!! Raymond stood up with great excitement. It all fell into place. In the twinkling of an eye he was back at the cave entrance at the Tower of the Flock.

"Of course, that stupendous light which enveloped this cave at the time of the birth of the Christ Child has to be the light that I must seek".

Then Raymond's thoughts returned to the Good Friday scene and the three hours darkness.

"Yes of course – the Nativity scene and the Crucifixion scene. The difference between birth and death. The vast contrast between Heavenly light and the darkness of Hell".

Raymond now wondered if the Cave of the Nativity could be the Holy of Holies. When he entered in, the scene before him was in stark contrast to what he had seen during his visit on that first holy Christmas Eve. Shepherds were busy helping ewes give birth to their lambs. New born lambs were being inspected for blemishes and defects. Those that were tainted in any way were rejected as unfit for Temple sacrifice. The much bleating and baaing that greeted the ears of Raymond and the sight of shepherds busy with their routine tasks of managing sheep and lambs led him to understand that the cave had now been returned to its mundane function as a birthing place for Temple lambs. This hardly appeared to Raymond to be the most likely setting for the Holy of Holies.

Raymond however kept his mind on the "light". The light that he had witnessed on Christmas Eve which had so mesmerised him did not originate from the Star of Bethlehem. That Star was at first a conjunction of Jupiter and Regulus. Finally it was Jupiter's retrograde motion which indicated from Jerusalem the city of the Saviour's Birth. The light around the cave had been completely different and emanating from a non-astronomical source.

"It must have something to do with the Shekinah. But what exactly is the Shekinah? It means of course 'the indwelling glory of God'. What other light could possibly shine at the time of the Incarnation when God Himself becomes a man?"

Once again Raymond tried to recover what remained of the vague memories of his religious education lessons – vague no doubt because of his then lack of interest and inattentiveness.

"The Shekinah light guided the Israelites on their way out of Egypt and into the Promised Land", a female voice was heard to say. "God lived with men. His dwelling place was in the Ark of the Covenant and the Shekinah glory lit up the way of the Israelites. The Shekinah glory was once more on Earth. The glory of the Son of God lightens the way for every man in this world." This was the voice of his old religious instructor, Mrs. Clayton.

Although he could not see her, Raymond begged her forgiveness for all the trouble he had caused her during those periods of religious instruction. He accused himself of pride and arrogance and acknowledged that he owed her a tremendous debt of gratitude.

That most longed for mist made its welcoming presence and Raymond was carried away. He wondered where he would be taken to by the divine powers which rule the Universe.

CHAPTER 11.

HOME AGAIN, HOME AGAIN.

A great joy came over Raymond. It was a joy he had never experienced at any time in his life. It was a joy surpassing all other joys. If this joy intensified, he felt he would die of it! Raymond was back in the control room of CERN!

He looked heavenwards and knelt down in prayer and thanksgiving. He wondered if it had all been a dream. Time would tell.

"Time!" thought Raymond. "Just exactly what is the time? How much time has passed since all of this happened".

He went over to the door and tried to open it. He could not. He pulled and heaved with all his might but that door just would not budge.

"What's wrong? What can the matter be?"

He fell back on a chair exhausted.

"Wow! I actually feel exhausted. In fact – I feel!" Raymond shouted excitedly.

All his normal bodily functions had been restored. He felt like a normal human being again.

He decided he would call out for his family.

"Ruth!, James! Can you hear me? Ruth! James. Come here!!". But there was no response.

Raymond walked down the centre of the control room where a small window was located. He looked out of it but saw absolutely nothing but blackness. He pressed his face on the glass, but the same blackness presented itself to him.

Raymond went back to his chair and pondered the situation. He noticed a kettle in a corner of the room.

"I haven't had a cup of tea in ….eh well ages! Quite literally ages."

Raymond made himself some tea. According to his own reckoning, his adventures had spanned around eighteen months. He had neither ate nor drank in all of that time. Oh how he enjoyed that cup of tea! He had never enjoyed tea so much.

When the ecstasy of drinking the tea was over, Raymond felt compelled to return to the window. As he concentrated more intensely on the blackness on the outside there was something that occurred to him as being somewhat peculiar – the lights from the inside of the room did absolutely nothing to lighten up the outside of the control room. And there was yet something else that occurred to Raymond, the blackness on the outside was exactly of the same quality as the darkness he had experienced when he had stood on the Temple Mount on the first Good Friday.

Raymond paced up and down the room. "There has to be some connection between that darkness and the darkness outside of this control room".

He came to the conclusion that the Earth was still stuck in a timeless Black Hole and that all that had been restored of the "currently former planet" was the CERN control room. It was clear to Raymond that his tasks were not over. He still had something more to do.

First of all he thought about the darkness without. Next he considered its opposite – the Shekinah light.

"Of course. It was by bombarding particles at the speed of light which brought about this horror. Restoration of time and matter can only be effected if I achieve a slowdown of light at minus 186,300 miles per second.

For hours, Raymond tried to figure out how he could possibly achieve this. He set the CERN apparatus in motion once more and started bombarding particles at the speed of light. Instead of gradually slowing the bombardment down, Raymond suddenly switched it off. The suddenness of this action achieved the speed of minus 186,300 miles per second.

The room shuddered and sent Raymond flying across it. He hit the back wall hard then fell on his face to the ground. He must have lain on the floor for around ten minutes before he found the strength to pick himself up. He slowly staggered over to the window. He proceeded to press his face against it. His eyes were closed. He was too frightened to open them as he was unsure of the spectacle which would present itself to him. All sorts of horrors passed through his mind. Had he landed in Hell? Was he eternally lost in space? Was he in another Universe? Perhaps in another dimension.

Gradually he opened his eyes. He breathed a great sigh of relief when he discovered that all the familiar surroundings external to the control room were there. He fell on his knees in thanksgiving and adoration for this deliverance.

When Raymond tried to exit from the control room, he found that once again he was prevented. The door was stuck fast.

"What now, what now?" he asked in desperation. "I've done everything I can".

He then heard the voice of his guardian angel say. "You have indeed done everything. What is required of you now is to understand the meaning of the final task you have just completed."

Once more Raymond entered into a long and deep

process of thought and reflection. One of the methods that Raymond had been taught to use during his period of training at Cambridge University was to ask relevant questions when trying to work out the solution to a mathematical problem.

His first question was: "Why should my understanding of what has happened have any relevance to the objective reality of what has been done?"

His instructors had told him that asking the question would help bring about the answer.

"It surely must relate to Quantum Mechanics. The observer has an affect on the thing observed".

Then came the second question: "What ensured that negative slowdown did not reduce to speeds infinitely slower than 186, 300 miles per second?"

After a few seconds of thought he asked the most obvious follow-on question. "What ensured that the speed which I achieved in my experiment did not exceed the speed of light?" Raymond reasoned that it must be the same process in both cases.

The fourth and most obvious question was: "What then is the process?".

Raymond started analysing things in the form of a mini-lecture he gave to himself.

"If anything achieves a speed which exceeds the speed of light and that that speed increases on an infinite basis then it ceases to be light. It can only be darkness. The gravitational pull of a Black Hole is such that not even light can escape from it. What then happens to the light inside a Black Hole? It must enter into infinite minus slowdown and create infinite darkness."

"Now by this analysis, should not infinite minus slowdown create something which is no longer darkness but light? It cannot because it would then have a positive speed of 186,300 miles per second which of course would contradict its infinite minus speed. Yet how can one be slower than stationary? In mathematics, negative numbers are theoretically possible. I have five apples, but in theory I can take away six. Now how would this work in physics? Let's call it 'negative speed'. I think it must be connected with gravity. The stronger the gravitational pull of a Black Hole, the more energy an object, in this case light, has to exert in order to achieve any speed. So let us say that the gravity in a given Black Hole is 2x and the speed of light is 1x then light will have to double its energy to escape the clutches of the Black Hole. But light cannot travel faster than light or else it wouldn't be light – so it can never escape the Black Hole. Yet gravity can be more powerful than light but something prevents it from being light" If light cannot travel faster than 186,300 miles per second, then negative slowdown cannot exceed minus 186,300 miles per second.

What exactly the mechanism was for this put Raymond into another bout of mental exertion. After about an hour, Raymond continued his lecture to his imaginary audience.

"Now an observer can only observe; he may even influence the results of the experiment, but he cannot create the laws of physics."

At this juncture Raymond stood frozen on the spot. "Cannot create the laws of physics": this phrase kept repeating itself in his mind again and again and again. It kept leaping out at him.

"NO!!! Indeed not", Raymond shouted out in great ecstasy. "But - a CREATOR CAN!!

The Shekinah light is the light which ensures against infinite darkness, an infinite darkness which is contained in natural light. That is why nothing can move faster than light. If it did it would not be light, and if it is not light it can only be darkness. The ultimate observer is God and He is not only an observer but a Creator and Sustainer. He is the one Who keeps light within the positive and negative parameters of 186,300 miles per second. Human observation gives mankind some share in influencing observations, but mankind cannot alter the laws of physics. This ties in with how we are created in the image of God but not in the exact likeness of God."

Raymond then thought about Heisenberg's Uncertainty Principle. He then recalled how Sir Fred Hoyle claimed in his Bampton series of lectures in 1967 that the uncertainty only arises from human imprecision in calculation but the Universe itself is very precise.

"The precision of the Universe .... The Anthropic Principle..... the fine tuning of the Universe for life". Raymond's mind was now working overtime. "Now add to this the fact that cosmologists understand the Universe in terms of mathematics...and yet....and yet....the emergence of life in terms of chance evolution defies the laws of mathematics. Didn't Hoyle calculate that the resources and age of the Universe were simply insufficient for evolution? Yes, he said that 'it is as if some super-intellect has been monkeying around with the laws of physics'. This brings me back to the Creator."

Raymond then turned to his own recent experiences.

"Now why was it necessary for me to be transported back to the time of the Incarnation for the Earth to be brought back to life and light?" Raymond thought about this for some time.

"As we've just seen, light captured in a Black Hole can never become light again, according to the laws of physics, as gravity can sometimes be stronger than the speed of light. But...if a super-intellect starts 'monkeying around' with those laws, then the darkness can become light. And Who is Christ but the Light of the World? God becomes man and darkness becomes light."

Then Raymond thought about how all this might relate to the Higgs Boson Particle. The Higgs Boson particle may or may not be discovered. I may be the one to discover it, on the other hand, I may not be. Yet, what I have discovered is far greater than any discovery ever made."

Raymond then stared up at the ceiling and simply said "thank you class, that is all for now".

A round of great applause then caused Raymond to suddenly lower his head. To his amazement, he found out that his class had not been so imaginary after all. There before him were an array of angels all singing their praises for his great wisdom. And right in the front row of this "class" were some "pupils" whose presence truly delighted Raymond – his mother, his father, Mrs. Clayton, Mr. Barclay, Sir Fred Hoyle, Albert Einstein, Nicolas Copernicus, Abbe Georges Lamaitre, Gregor Mendel and Michael Faraday. After two minutes of great acclamation, the "class' disappeared from his sight.

Raymond now went over to the door. This time it opened.

CHAPTER 12.

CHRISTMAS AT CERN.

Professor Raymond Davidson was an utterly exhausted man. He felt that his legs could not support him any longer.

"Ruth, James!!", he called out.

His wife and son soon appeared. As they saw Raymond collapse onto his knees, their walk gave way to a run.

"Raymond darling! Oh my goodness, are you all right? What has happened?", cried Ruth.

"Dad, what's wrong. Oh Dad!" exclaimed James.

Raymond looked up at his wife and son with tired and tear-filled eyes. "I.. I ... wasn't sure if you'd still be here."

Mother and son looked at each other in total bewilderment.

"I'm.. I'm...I'm just so sorry I've been away for these past eighteen months", he said apologetically to them.

"What are you talking about Raymond?", his wife asked.

"You've only been away for ten minutes Dad", his son added.

James helped his father out of the complex and into the car. Ruth drove back to their villa.

"Shall I get a doctor?", Ruth suggested.

"No", said Raymond firmly. "I just need rest. I'll explain everything in the morning."

The following day, Raymond told his wife and son everything that had happened to him.

At the end of his account Raymond told his family: "I'll not only be accompanying you to church every Sunday from now on, but I'm going to embark upon part-time studies for the priesthood and seek ordination. Your grandfather was absolutely right James – science and religion are not in conflict with each other, they complement each other."

Later that evening the family attended Midnight Mass. When they were driving home, James suggested to his father that it could all have just been a dream.

"Now you're the one who's doubting James – wasn't it always me who was the atheist?"

As the Davidson family entered their home they noticed something peculiar. James looked ahead at the living-room door and noticed a bright light coming from it.

"What is that?" asked his wife somewhat startled.

"Maybe it's burglars", said James.

The three of them approached the living-room with great caution. When they entered, the light completely enveloped them. For about a minute they could see nothing. When the light dimmed, they found themselves outside the entrance of the cave at the Tower of the Flock. Ruth and James were too awe-struck to say anything. The three of them walked over to the cave and saw the Infant Jesus with Mary His mother and St. Joseph his foster-father. The animals were there and the shepherds came to adore their new-born king. Fifteen minutes later they were back in their living-room at their home in Switzerland .

"Dad! I'm.. I'm so sorry I doubted your story", said James feeling rather ashamed.

"Don't worry son. God dispelled your doubt by allowing

you and your mother to witness a scene from the greatest story ever told".

On Christmas morning, Raymond got a phone call from one of his colleagues at CERN.

"Raymond, you'd better get over here pronto. And bring Ruth and James too."

"I feel something has gone terribly wrong at the complex", said a worried Raymond as he drove with his family to the CERN reactor..

"I can't understand why they want to involve us in it", said Ruth. "James and I are not scientists and we cannot be held responsible for any technical hitches with the collider".

"Any damage done is entirely my fault", Raymond assured his family. "I take full responsibility".

A delegation of CERNs senior scientists awaited the arrival of the Davidson family.

"What's going on here?" asked Raymond with great concern.

"Let's go to the control room", said one of his colleagues.

"What is this all about? And why do you involve my family?"

When they were standing outside the control room the same colleague said: "before we go inside, I just want to ask you if what is in there is your idea of a practical joke?"

"What ARE you talking about?", asked Raymond.

The control room door was opened. To his amazement, Raymond and his family found it to be full of Christmas decorations. There was a massive fir tree in one corner complete with lights, tinsel and star. Holly, ivy and mistletoe were all around the room. A table was laid out with the most magnificent array of turkey, pheasant, goose and all the Christmas trimmings.

Raymond knew what had happened. It was all part of

the amazing and wonderful experiences he had recently undergone.

"I can understand your taste for the Christmas fare", said another of his colleagues, "but this display under the Christmas tree seems to be rather out of character for you?"

Raymond caste his eyes to the foot of the great tree. He hadn't noticed it. It was the nativity scene – and it was just like the one he and his family had gazed upon when they were at the Tower of the Flock.

"Well, thanks a million Ray", said another of the scientists. But.. eh… if I might ask…where did all this come from?!!"

Raymond looked at his family, then at his colleagues and simply replied: "let's just say that it's all part of the miracle of Christmas!"